ACKNOWLEDGMENTS

I am grateful for all of the opportunities that have come my way. I continue to pray for many blessings to fall in my lap. Thank you, supporters and readers. Thank you for reading my work, sharing a link or suggest my book to someone. Special thanks to my mentors who I will not name for the continuous support and encouragement.

Thank you, Boss Lady, aka, Patrice Williams, better known as National Best-Selling Author, Mz. Lady P. You have guided, encouraged, and never given up on me, and I appreciate it. For two years, I have learned so much as an author from you on how to promote and brand myself. Your hard work and dedication do not go unnoticed, nor do I take you for granted. I look forward to growing and becoming the dopiest author I can be under your company. You are stuck me FOREVER! LOL, you are a beast in this industry so to be a part of your team is a wonderful feeling. Thank you for seeing the potential in me during a difficult time in my life.

Shout out to my dope pen sisters and brother. Our family is growing and glowing with talent across the board. I'm proud of you all. Thank you for always keeping it real and for providing advice and motivation. This is the sixth book that I have completed, and it is an amazing feeling. I want to thank my mother as she watches from heaven and continues to give me inspiration. There is not one day that goes by that I do not think about you. You inspire some of my crazy characters from the stories you used to share about back in the day. Continue to watch over your son and me.

To those who have a dream, follow it and never give up! Push through, and if you want it bad enough, your hard work will pay off. The stories I write always have some type of message to it, and it is my sincere hope that it inspires the readers. Living the life, we were dealt is easier said than done for some folks. Therefore, it is nice to get lost in others' drama via a good book. Each character created is based on friends, old associates, and from people watching.

Lastly, I would like to acknowledge myself for fighting against depression. Each day is a challenge, especially during November and December. The loss of a mother is a hard pill to swallow. Depression can consume and turn you into a different person unless you fight it! I write to cope, I write to inspire, and I write to promote my story.

Love yours truly,

Sweet Tee

NOTE FROM THE AUTHOR

My inspiration for this novella came from a combination of watching television shows, browsing Facebook, and doing research on pastors who have dealt with infidelity and imperfect marriages. Often the top three reasons a spouse claims they cheated are because they felt neglected, lack of communication, and it just happened. It got me to thinking about different scenarios and how couples let outside things interfere with their relationships. In tradition, marriage is a bond shared between two people and God. Nowadays everyone and they mama are involved via social media, which leads to more separation instead of unity.

As a single person, I have no idea what marriage is like, nor do I wish to at this point in my life. Please, don't get me wrong. I am a firm believer in black love because there is nothing more beautiful than to see a couple in love. However, the other side of the picture isn't always perfect.

Get ready to meet Michelle, a woman who tried to be the perfect wife and pastor yet got the short end of the stick. Her marriage to Jacob appeared to be perfect. They were the godly couple everyone loved. However, her dedication to the church caused the man she said "I do" to betray her trust and step out of their marriage. This book is a reminder that every couple, including pastors battle with physical and emotional infidelity.

EVERY SAINT HAS A SECRET

A NOVELLA

SWEET TEE

KEEP UP WITH SWEET TEE

Facebook: Authoress Sweet Tee
   Readers Group: Sweet Tee's Reading Corner
   Instagram: sweettee3215
   Twitter: AuthoressSweetT
   Website: http://jonestt25.wixsite.com/sweettee

SYNOPSIS

From the outside looking in, the Thomas' appear to be the perfect couple of the church. Meet forty-three-year-old Pastor Michelle Thomas, married to big-time television host Jacob Thomas. Jacob was one of the highest paid Christian hosts in the region. He also served as reverend before his switch to television.

Michelle took her calling to serve God and the congregation seriously, so much so that she began to neglect her husband. One September evening she decided to pop up at CNT studio to surprise him with dinner. Nothing could have prepared her for what she witnessed upon her arrival. That night she learned that Jacob had more than scripts on his desk. Shocked and hurt, she refused to let the devil disturb her peace.

As time moved forward another secret of Jacob's came to light testing her faith. Will she be the forgiving wife and woman of the cloth, or will she turn into a woman scorned? Get ready for a story of faith, karma, and forgiveness.

PROLOGUE

JACOB THOMAS

S eptember 2017

"Oh yes, Zahara. Just like that! I love the way you release my stress and give me good love."

Jacob had the young woman over the desk partaking in an activity meant for husband and wife. Half dressed; his pants were down and around his ankles exposing his bare, toned butt cheeks.

"I'm yours, Jacob! You never let me down." Zahara worked her back over time until they both let out a faint sound simultaneously.

Wrapped up in each other's pleasures, neither of them realized Michelle had quietly pushed the door open. She had witnessed the entire sex scene that they had just performed. For five minutes, Michelle stood horrified as Jacob committed adultery. The sound of the plate crashing to the ground caused Jacob and Zahara to look in her direction.

"This is why you couldn't make it home for dinner? You are a sorry ass!" Michelle shouted surprised at the words that left from her lips.

"MICHELLE, please let me explain!" he shouted while he scrambled to pull up his boxers and pants in one motion.

"Save it, Jacob," Michelle hissed as the tears rolled down her face.

The hurt in her face was undeniable as Jacob did his best to ignore it because he got caught.

Zahara used the opportunity to get out as she quickly stepped over the food and plate. Michelle glanced in the woman's direction then diverted her eyes back to her husband in disgust. She turned to walk away as Jacob tried to talk and gently grabbed her arm. Beyond pissed to no return, Michelle did her best to avoid his touch.

"You better get your hand-" she started through gritted teeth as he quickly released his grip. The entire time he followed alongside her down the short distance from his office to the hallway.

All he could do is watch the backside of his wife storm out the double doors of the building. Filled with mixed emotions, he stood in the middle of the room embarrassed by the event. A handful of his colleagues had just witnessed a scandalous quarrel but quickly diverted their attention elsewhere.

Jacob went back into his office and closed the door. He paced the floor back and forth waiting for a bright idea to pop in his head. He cleaned up the mess from the floor giving Michelle time to get home and cool off. Thirty minutes later, he quietly came out of hiding and slowly emerged from behind his door. Since everyone had moved to another area of the building, Jacob was able to slip out unnoticed. He ran to the parking garage and climbed inside his Mercedes Benz truck.

He pulled into the driveway erratically not bothering to even park in the garage. Greeted with silence, Jacob entered the home. He slowly walked through the foyer and continued on the first floor towards the chef style kitchen. That is when he noticed the flames from the patio area. Hesitant to take the steps outside, Jacob risked it and opened the double patio doors.

"Michelle, please let me-," he tried to address her, but her hand went up stopping him. The moment he moved closer, he couldn't believe what his eyes were witnessing. The flames from the fire pit were burning his clothes and belongings.

"I know those are not my three-thousand-dollar suites?! Oh hell no not the Ferragamo shoes!" Jacob yelled horrified. Without a word, she just stood there, tossed a few more items in the fire, and sipped her wine. On that night she wasn't a pastor, no, she was a woman scorned out for revenge.

Jacob retreated with his tail tucked between his legs and went up to their suite. He retrieved his belongings shoving things in a duffle bag. He stormed out without a word because there was nothing to say. He didn't want to be the next thing on fire. Caught in action, literally, Jacob had no one to blame. He went back downstairs and straight out the door as he shook his head. At the driver's door, he tossed his bag in the seat and got inside. Contemplating his next move, he had two options. He could go to a hotel for a few days or call Zahara. Deep down in his spirit, Jacob knew going to the hotel was the best thing to do.

In a cloudy phase, Jacob didn't realize he had started his car and drove across town. It wasn't until he had parked and turned the engine off that he became fully aware of his surroundings. Zahara's 2017 navy blue Lincoln Continental sat parked in her driveway. From his seat he leaned forward able to see her living room light on, prompting him to get out the truck. Jacob decided to leave his duffle bag just in case she rejected his entry to her home.

As he walked along the path that led to her front entrance, flashbacks from earlier darted in his head. He pressed the doorbell then stood patiently and waited. Finally, the door slowly opened as she stood with a hand on her hip. Wearing a nightgown that barely made it to her knees, Jacob couldn't do anything but gawk. He imagined seeing her with nothing on, her glistening perfect sculptured coco brown body.

"Oh, look. The wife put you out and now here you are. Do you know how embarrassed I was when she walked in on us?" Zahara asked waiting for an answer as she shifted her weight to one side and folded her arms. Not able to forgive him so quickly, she wanted him to sweat a little as payback.

"I'm sorry. We both were careless and should have waited until later to be intimate. Let me come inside so that we can discuss this further behind closed doors."

Silent for a minute, Zahara played hard to get as she kept him waiting outside. Eventually the frowned face she wore softened to a submissive smile, and she invited him inside.

TWO MONTHS HAD PASSED, and the pair lived together as if they were a newlywed. They had more sex than usual, which caused Jacob to fall head over hills. Feeling free, he finally had what he wanted. However, what he received in the aftermath changed everything. Around eight at night, Jacob arrived home from a long day of conducting counseling sessions. All he wanted to do was strip, shower, eat, and relax. To his surprise, she cooked steak, baked potatoes, and a side salad.

"Hey baby, I'm glad you're home!" Zahara said with an unusual smile. She had literally just placed the juicy, sizzling pieces of meat on the restaurant style plate.

"Wow, honey, the food smells good!" He greeted her with a soft kiss to the forehead. The moment he took a seat at the table, he noticed the small-sized gift box that sat on the table.

"No!" Zahara yelled. "Don't open it yet. I want you to enjoy your meal first; it was made with love, so you must eat it while hot."

"Okay if you insist. Can you pass the Italian dressing?"

She passed it per his request as they shared stories about their day. The entire time Jacob seemed to be in a good mood, and Zahara relied on that mood to transfer when he found out the surprise. A half hour later, curiosity piqued his interest, prompting him to lift the lid. Watching on nervously, she studied Jacob's face for a reaction as he stared at the content. It included two First Response pregnancy tests.

"WHAT!" The opened mouth and wide eyes were a sign that he was just as surprised as Zahara when she found out.

In shock, he removed himself from the table and disappeared to the living room area. Zahara followed behind him and took a seat on the sofa. She watched him pace back and forth. Obviously, she had mixed emotions as well. Not ready to be a mother, she didn't know how to move forward. A few deep breaths in, she slowly exhaled before she responded.

"Jacob I'm not ready to be a mother nor did I want it to happen this way. Bringing a baby in the world is serious business, are you ready for that challenge?"

"I understand this entire situation didn't pan out the way you wanted it to, but we will get through this. The last thing we need is for Michelle to find out." He tried to believe his own words, but he knew the church folks would have a grand time gossiping. It wasn't fair to Michelle.

"How did we let this happen?" he asked aloud, throwing his hands in the air out of confusion. "We used condoms.

"Jacob, please take a seat. You're making me nervous. He did just that. He sat down beside her and grabbed her hand. He dropped his head in his hands, then raised it back up, and turned his body to face her.

"Zahara, what we have is special. I know that our relationship isn't ideal, me being married and all. I am sorry. You deserve so much better. Can I really give you what you deserve?"

His sincere question made her bust out in tears as she leaned over and laid her head on him. He consoled her as the news marinated in his head that a baby was on the way. Jacob never really wanted children, nor did he feel like the paternal type of man. The thought of raising a child scared him for obvious reasons, but most importantly because he wasn't ready. Both a blessing and a curse, Jacob had to figure out how to move forward. He said a silent prayer for his wife. He knew delivering the news to her would be devastating.

1

MICHELLE THOMAS

Several Months Earlier

Michelle performed two personal baptisms, conducted Bible study, and went for her daily visit to the hospital within the course of Wednesday. Finally, able to sit still for a while, she sat in her swivel chair and glanced over the calendar. She was amazed at all of the things she did in a given day. No matter the task, she tackled it until it was complete.

As the female pastor of Temple Faith EMC, her duties were never done, and before Jacob stepped down from the pulpit, he too shared some of those responsibilities. Nevertheless, she continued to lead as the sole pastor, giving her all. Her latest frustration involved thoughts about the neighborhood kids. Michelle brainstormed ways to keep the kids from hanging around the local store, a popular spot to get drugs and other items.

Michelle became so devoted to her church that her home life didn't exist. It had been so long since she had a weekend alone with Jacob. His schedule entailed early nights and early mornings. He had to be at the TV studio before dawn. Sometimes Michelle wished married life were easier than it seemed in the movies. Although there were things in dire need of attention in her marriage, the love she had for her husband never changed. One look at him made her nerves calm, uncertainty vanished, and the butterflies in her stomach were genuine.

Never ending duties kept her so busy sometimes that she didn't know which day of the week it was without a calendar. Still young so to speak, Michelle made sure to work out on a regular basis. Pressures and responsibility could wear a person down. Thus Michelle stayed committed to her treadmill.

BEFORE SHE DELIVERED her sermon each Sunday, she tended to look out into the crowd in search for Jacob's face. He made her feel at ease whenever she stood behind the pulpit. For over five years, Michelle stood and preached the word to the same loyal two hundred members of Temple Faith. Many men doubted her success as a female pastor. Over time, she proved she could lead the congregation just as good as a man could. Take her husband Jacob, for example. He used to lead worship with Michelle for three years. When he stepped down from the pulpit to pursue another calling, Michelle became the head pastor.

After service, two women who wanted to tell her personally how much they enjoyed her sermon greeted Michelle. The women were older and had been members before Michelle became pastor. Amid them approaching, Jacob had also walked up trying not to interrupt. Mrs. Lee directed her attention to them both.

"Pastor Thomas, you are a lucky man to have such a wonderful wife who can preach her tail off. Chile, the Lord knew what he was doing using you to be his disciple," she said, tapping each of them on the arm.

"Yes, ma'am, I truly am blessed to have her," Jacob replied to Mrs. Lee who didn't take her eyes off the pair.

"Thank you, Mrs. Lee, for the kind words! I'm just glad I'm the vessel," Michelle responded. The four smiled at each other as the women slowly went their separate ways.

Jacob followed behind Michelle to the side room/office where she kept her robes, communion stuff, and extra hymn books. He informed her he had to leave early due to a work-related obligation but would see her later. Before leaving, he placed his hands on each side of her head and kissed her forehead. Kisses to the forehead were the best type of kiss to Michelle, as she felt safe and loved.

She stood still, stuck in the moment until Jacob disappeared before she snapped back to reality. A quick glance at her watch prompted her to move a little faster so that she wouldn't be late to adult bible study. It wasn't a good look for the pastor to be late to her own class.

Adult Bible study ended around two o'clock, and by then most everyone had already left the church. Michelle stayed an extra hour to check her voicemail messages and to prep for confirmation class. This session's seven young people dedicated one hour every Monday to attending confirmation class with the goal to become closer to God. It warmed Michelle's heart to have the chance to work with so many talented children who loved the Lord as she did. She stuffed the seven folders with materials for class then left her office and out the building.

WHEN SHE WALKED through the door from the garage entrance, a fresh vase of roses sat on the kitchen counter with a card next to it. Surprised by Jacob's small gesture, it made her feel warm inside. Not bothering to look at the card, she headed up the stairs to the bedroom. Jacob wasn't there, so she went back downstairs. She slid the card from the red Hallmark envelope and opened it. Smiling, she silently read it.

Hey, beautiful,

Sorry I couldn't be here when you got home. Please accept these roses! I'll be at the studio working so it might be late when I make it home.

Love, JT

In awe the smile never left her face, but it didn't keep her from wondering why they hadn't made love in the past two weeks. Yes, she'd gained a few extra pounds, but it wasn't sloppy weight. Still early in the day, Michelle went to her room and changed from her church clothes into workout gear. There was a treadmill located in the basement that she frequently used three times per week. Cardio helped her decompress from the mental exhaustion she experienced.

The workout did her some justice, but when she stepped under the wide stainless-steel showerhead, nothing mattered. Strong bursts of water flowed and beat over her bronze skin. The lathered body wash rinsed off her along with the troubles of the day. Michelle stepped outside the shower as a cold gush air whooshed over her. She quickly wrapped herself in a soft Supima cotton bath towel and dried off. Michelle rubbed on lotion and dressed in an Alpaca relaxed fit jogging suit.

Afterwards, she made her way to the spotless kitchen that hadn't been used in a few days. She retrieved some mini carrots and celery with ranch dip and sipped bottled water. Feeling the burn and aftermath of her workout, she enjoyed sitting down in peace. The rest of the evening went by fast as she spent time reading and blogging on the church's social media pages. Usually, someone at the church managed all the social media pages. However, she felt the need to post a personal message on Twitter.

Pastor Michelle@ Temple Faith EMC

At the end of the day when you are alone, use that time to reflect on your day and what you did. Did you help someone? Give a compliment? Did you perform one act of kindness to someone who was less fortunate than you? If you answered yes, then continue to do the work of our Lord. If you answered no, don't be ashamed; just find a way to do better! We are all servants of the Lord.

2

ZAHARA HUDSON

A cup of Chamomile tea later, Zahara felt better. However, she still didn't understand why Jacob couldn't stay the night. After all, he'd practically lived with her. He decided to go home in effort to keep the peace at home. Although she never envied Michelle, she did anytime Jacob had to leave. Catching feelings for another woman's husband hadn't been the plan. Nevertheless, falling in love was something she couldn't change.

Never confronted personally by Michelle, Zahara enjoyed every second spent with Jacob. As his personal assistant at the television station, she had the best of both worlds. She saw his milk chocolate chiseled body up close and personal every day.

She knew all too well, how to use her assets to get what she wanted. At sixteen, she had the shape of a twenty-year-old woman, C-cup breasts, and an apple bottom behind. Mature for her age, she got many men in trouble from her mere appearance, and their gawking stares. Nothing she did in the past was as bad as what she had been doing for two years. Sleeping with a married man was a new low for her. She lived on the wild side and didn't feel bad about her actions.

At the young age of seven, her mother's lewd behavior wasn't the typical actions a parent should've shown a little girl. Growing up, she soaked up everything she saw her mother do. The older she got, the more she understood the reasons behind her mother's actions. It was Zahara's observation that men did almost anything to get a woman's panties off. Flirting became her specialty, which is eventually how she lured Jacob.

Aware of the consequences, the affair between her and Jacob Thomas was unavoidable. The pair mashed together like hands in gloves back in 2015 when Jacob became Zahara's counselor. He had just taken a break from preaching and wanted to utilize his degree and license in addiction and spiritual counseling. Never was it her intentions to get involved with him, as he served only as her voice of reason. Counseling made her more balanced and in return, Jacob became more and more attractive. Each session their bond strengthened the more she opened up. Her vulnerability also opened the door to their conversations going astray.

By October 2016, their hour-long professional sessions turned into Jacob disclosing issues about his marriage. He got so comfortable talking it seemed as if she was the counselor. She found herself watching his lips as he talked. Only lustful thoughts invaded her head of how she wanted to bite his bottom lip. That's when the three-person relationship started. The only problem, Michelle was the third party left in the dark.

Life began to get more complicated with each session the two had until he made the first move. To console Zahara, he held her hand, which led to his hand caressing her face and other body parts. She was unable to resist the soft touch from a man she had spilled her guts to make her weak, a rule breaker. She did a slight lean in to show the visual crease in her breasts. One gesture prompted fifteen minutes of long overdue hot and heavy lustful sex.

THREE SNOOZE BUTTONS LATER, the bright sun rays blinded Zahara, causing her to squint. Surprised it had already been ten-thirty in the morning, she felt thankful to sleep late for a change. Her reading addiction kept her up past midnight or later. She climbed out of her comfortable bed in a shuffle motion right into the bathroom. Glad to enjoy a day off. She went down to the kitchen to put water on for a cup of Chai tea. Out of habit, she swung open the refrigerator and stared at the contents inside. Nothing satisfied the craving she had for something finger licking good. After tea, she went back to her bedroom.

Too lazy to cook, Zahara didn't want to eat alone, so she called her sister India while she dressed and told her to drive to Panera Bread. Of course, India agreed and texted the moment she got in the car to drive off. Food brought them together no matter the weather. She lived near a variety of popular restaurants, which was a good and bad thing.

The sisters bonded over a combination of lunch and sweets. India noticed how fast her sister smashed the small plate of mini blueberry muffins. Zahara hated blueberries, so it seemed weird that she ate practically all of them.

"Oh, my goodness! Sis, you knocked up."

"What the hell you talking about? I think that muffin got you trippin'," she tried to deny the comment.

"Since when do you eat Swiss cheese or blueberries? I'll wait." A natural smartass, India waited for her sister's answer.

"Ever hear of trying new things and period cravings?"

"I'm not trying to be all in your business or whatnot, but if you are expecting, it's time to make some serious decisions."

"Damn, I thought I was the oldest," Zahara blurted as she put her hand on India's. "Drop it, sis. Alright?"

"Okay. I'll leave it alone," India agreed. Zahara knew it was a possibility she could be pregnant.

No longer able to take another bite, the sisters were stuffed. Per paying the bill, Zahara requested medium sized Styrofoam to-go containers for their leftovers. Still early she suggested getting a mani and pedi at a nearby nail shop, of course, India accepted. Nailtique was a nice little spot, and the owners were down to earth. Their recent move to a bigger space made it even more of a popular place.

Luckily for the sisters, two nail techs had open seats and assisted then right away.

Self-care was one thing that Zahara believed in, especially since the TV station took up a lot of time. Sister time gave them a sense of connecting with each other since Jacob had moved in. Before that, India used to spend time at the house and stay over a few nights at a time. Things changed which caused a disconnect at times between the sisters, but their bond was unbreakable.

When Zahara made it home, she kicked off her shoes at the door. She then strolled to the kitchen and placed the Styrofoam container in the fridge and grabbed a bottled water before the door slammed shut. Stuffed she decided to take a quick nap so that she could be refreshed to fix dinner for her and Jacob. During her nap, she tossed and turned as if something or someone had haunted her.

3

JACOB THOMAS

Living in sin with Zahara was a sure way of putting a stamp on Jacob's application to hell for committing adultery. He'd been laying his head in two homes. Loving someone other than his spouse prompted him to do stupid things like jeopardize years of marriage and stability. As a pastor himself, life was far from normal, which is why he went into the counseling field. He knew right from wrong, but his manhood stirred him down the wrong road. Sex outside of marriage tended to be something men struggled to fight.

Unhappy in his marriage, Jacob went about handling it in an unhealthy sinful way. As a pastor and husband, he committed vows and made promises that he had broken to both God and his wife. No man was perfect, including him, and every day he was a work in progress. The love he had for his wife hadn't changed, but the sexual connection wasn't there anymore. No sparks or stimulation occurred between them, which had become more of an issue for him. A man had needs and urges that needed to be fulfilled by a woman.

There was never a good enough excuse to cheat on your spouse, whether a man or woman. Jacob began to feel those cheating urges almost a year after he stepped down from the pulpit. He then got recertified to conduct counseling sessions a few days a week. As a spiritual counselor, he had five clients, and one of those individuals was a woman. Yes, it was Zahara, his current side chick. Jacob never intended to cross any lines, but it happened.

It grew hard being married to a woman who made more time for the church than her husband. He understood her vow to serve God and God's people without question, however, her neglecting him was the main cause for his infidelity. He wasn't the first man of the cloth to cheat and sure wouldn't be the last one. Jacob tried to remember the good times he and Michelle shared and wondered how things went wrong. They used to laugh and joke and even practice sermons together.

Careful not to wake Zahara, Jacob prepared for bed. He went into the bathroom to brush his teeth. In the process, he stopped and stared at himself in the mirror. The man who appeared back at him wasn't the same person a few years ago. He took a deep look at his reflection and let out a deep sigh.

"Lord what am I doing? Show me the way," he said aloud.

Conflicted in thought, he brushed his teeth, rinsed, and shut off the light. Headed into the bedroom, Jacob pulled the covers back and slid underneath. Zahara moved closer to him in a spooning position, which shortly turned, into an after-hours sex session.

HALF SLEEP the next morning Jacob ran around like a chicken with its head cut off. He tried to get ready for work but was off his game. Unsure how to fix it, Zahara tried to calm him down a bit.

"Zahara, have you seen my iPad charger?" he asked as he searched around for the white cord.

"No. It's around here somewhere," she answered.

"I need it and will not have time to stop and buy one. I have Tamela and David Mann appearing on the show, and all of my questions are saved on this device." He continued to double check his bag again when it suddenly dropped to the floor.

"Honey you need to slow down and take a deep breath," she insisted as she placed a hand on his chest. He stood in place and listened carefully to her voice.

"You are moving too fast, and it's making you go crazy. Take a few more deep breaths. You got this don't worry." Zahara did her best to give Jacob a pep talk to calm his nerves.

It had been a solid month since he Jacob had partially moved in with Zahara. He a foot in her door and the home he shared with Michelle. He tried his best to keep up his appearance. No one knew about the situation except the three individuals involved. Pretending to be perfect in the eyes of those who praised him grew difficult on Jacob and Zahara. Living a double life proved hard even for the smoothest man who managed to juggle two women.

"You're right," he agreed as he took a few deep breaths. Once he regained his composure, he grabbed his items ready to head out the door.

"I'll see you soon, baby," he said then kissed Zahara on the lips just as he stepped outside.

He climbed inside the truck but didn't drive off right away. Instead, he recited a morning prayer to help get him through the day. He proceeded to plug in his iPad to ensure it was fully charged before he stepped on the gas pedal.

Fifteen minutes until Showtime Jacob rehearsed his lines a few more times while everyone took their places. His assistant and lover Zahara made sure his coffee cup was filled with orange juice while he inserted the clear earpiece. The day had finally come for him to meet the Mann's and his mind wasn't clear enough. Jacob recited another prayer hoping to get rid of his jitters.

The topic for discussion was on forgiveness, keeping the faith, and living the word daily. The Mann's were the perfect couple to have on the show because they were very humble and down to earth. Their marriage had been a true testimony that black love still existed.

Jacob wondered how they managed to keep things together. During the show, they got through a list of questions, but most of the conversation turned into impromptu. The natural vibe between everyone made Jacob forget they were on television.

The interaction between the Mann's triggered a memory in which Jacob reflected when he and Michelle would sit and hold hands and stare endlessly into each other's eyes. Those were the happiest times they shared back when their love was fresh and new. The memories continued to flood his mind until he felt warm inside. The sound of the countdown back from a commercial grabbed his attention. The show continued for ten more minutes before the cameras were turned off. Jacob thanked his guests for blessing CNT and taking time out of their schedule. Afterwards he went to his office to work on the script for the next show. It made things easier for him when he arrived in the mornings.

ABOUT TO WALK through the door of the place he'd been shacking up, Jacob's phone rang. He retrieved it from his coat pocket to scan the screen before answering.

"Huh," he exhaled.

"Hi, honey. How you are doing?" he faked, not really concerned.

"I'm fine, just busy per usual. I'll be late tonight, but there is food in the fridge to warm up."

"Aww thank you. I'm working late too. Some of our guests for next week's lineup have canceled. We're trying to find replacements and all that jazz."

"Wow sorry to hear that. I'll let you go now. See you later, baby. Love you," she stated.

"Love you too," he responded as guilt punched him in the gut. Jacob tucked the phone back inside his pocket and walked inside Zahara's home.

Hours later he made it home to find his wife sound asleep. On his side of the bed, Jacob laid thinking about life, all the wrong he had done, and the guilt that stirred inside. Michelle beside him, the two remained silent as the sounds of their breathing filled the room. Unable to doze off, he tossed and turned. His dirty ways had blocked his ability to rest peacefully. He pondered if Michelle suspected he'd been cheating, and if so, why hadn't she confronted him yet. Blinking in the dark, he thought about his recent actions and wondered why he did the things he did. By the time he got sleepy, it was time to get up for work.

4

MICHELLE THOMAS

During Michelle's run on the treadmill, she couldn't help but think about the young lady India who didn't believe in God. It boggled her brain that the young lady had so many doubts. Something inside her wondered about the young girl she sat with in the sanctuary. Three miles later, she stopped the machine and headed for the shower. Afterwards she dressed in her clergy clothing ready to start her busy yet blessed day.

Right before eight o'clock, she strolled inside the church like she did every day smiling and ready to serve. On the way to her office, Tracy greeted and handed her a stack of mail. That girl had been a godsend and the best assistant Michelle ever had.

"Morning, Pastor Thomas! Looking wonderful as usual," Tracy complimented

"Morning dear! Thank you. If only I could clone you, darling. Please allow thirty minutes to pass before anyone requests to see me. I've got lots of emails to skim through among other stuff."

"Got it!"

Michelle glanced at the envelopes while she strolled to her office. She opened and closed the door and continued behind her executive bow front U-desk. She sat in the cushioned swivel chair, tossed the mail and handbag on the empty part of the desk. The first thing she did was check the church's email. There had to be over one hundred of them. Most of them were from other pastors and individuals who wanted to be listed on the prayer list.

Halfway through the emails, she decided to break. She minimized the window and opened another tab in Google and typed YouTube. A few clicks and strokes of the keys she found the video of her husband. It had been very rare that she tuned into his show on account of her schedule. Eyes glued to the screen she watched her husband in action. His message touched on forgiveness, something she believed in all too well. A knock at the door diverted her attention. She glanced at the digital clock that read eight-thirty.

"Come in," she announced.

"Good morning. Pastor Thomas do you have a quick second?" Deacon Jones asked.

She raised a hand to invite him in to take a seat while her hand closed her HP laptop. Michelle swiveled her chair to face him, removed her black framed Prada glasses from her face, and gave him her undivided attention.

"How can I assist you, deacon?" Michelle questioned staring him down like he was a tall, handsome piece of chocolate cake she wanted to stick her fork in.

"What I need to share with you is out of confidence, between the two of us. Is that something you can agree to?"

Michelle sat back in the chair and locked her fingers in front of her. She wondered what type of information deacon had to share that was so top secret. In agreement, she sat back up.

"Okay, whatever you tell me will not leave this office. You have my word." Her words sounded truthful as she gave him her undivided attention.

"At the end of the month, I will need to submit my transfer papers to Destiny Temple. This is the best decision for me to avoid the temptations I've been experiencing."

"Oh no, why? Is there anything I can do to change your mind?" Michelle asked in a concerned tone.

"Actually... Um, don't take this the wrong way, but you are part of the problem." His statement caused her to gasp with a confused stare. "What I mean is, I'm attracted to you, and it is inappropriate. Therefore I need to transfer."

His poor eye contact and constant fidgeting in the chair served as a giveaway that he was nervous. She never had a man come to her in the manner he did. Unsure what to say, Michelle said the first thing that came to her mind.

"Oh wow, this is the first time I've ever had anyone come to me with this type of issue. Please forgive me, I never intended for you to be in an uncomfortable environment. I'll sign whatever paperwork you need me too."

"Wonderful. I prayed there would be no hard feelings. I truly hope you understand my position. Galatians 5:16 would best describe my situation," Deacon Jones said. He stood to his feet while he gazed at her.

"We all must do what is necessary to avoid temptation, no explanation needed. I'll pray for you and your future at our sister church."

"Thank you. I will let you get back to work. Have a blessed day," he said before making his way out of her office.

In disbelief, Michelle let out a sigh and shook her head unable to forget Deacon Jones' words. For as long as she had known him it never occurred to her that's how he felt. Some men made it known when they were interested in a woman. Deacon Jones appeared to be different and had been good at hiding his feelings and emotions. She continued her tasks then stepped away from the desk momentarily. Half the time Michelle preached and the other half she pastored, both time consuming yet rewarding.

NOTHING COULD HAVE PREPARED Michelle for the set of events that took place after Sunday service. Each week she tried her best to memorize certain portions of her sermon, but Deacon Jones had messed her head up. While she stood at the pulpit, he sat to the left of her. She stumbled over a few words but was able to pull it together right up to the choir selection. When the service was over, and folks dispersed, Michelle removed her robe and hung it in the office. Out of the blue, there was a loud outburst.

"PASTOR! COME QUICK! YOU WON'T BELIEVE THIS!" Denise yelled hysterically. She was the financial ministry assistant.

Michelle's heart pounded as she silently prayed and followed Denise to the basement of the women's restroom. A teen couple was together doing the nasty.

"My word, what in the devil?" Michelle blurted out.

"Pastor we-" they tried to explain as she busted in on them and closed the door behind her.

"GET IN A STALL AND GET DRESSED. NOW!" Michelle shouted. Unable to think straight she felt like a parent who had just found her daughter with a boy. She continued. "Do you have any idea how disappointed I am in you two? This is a church for Christ sake."

"I don't know what to say other than I'm sorry. We did something very stupid," the young man acknowledged.

The teens finally showed their faces, and Michelle was appalled to find Kia and David, two of her best confirmation students. She never thought they could do something so drastic.

"Are we in trouble? Please don't tell my auntie," Kia pleaded.

"Right now, you can get out and go say a prayer. We'll discuss your punishment tomorrow after confirmation class."

Michelle slowly slung opened the door. With the coast clear and no one around, the three exited. She headed to her office in the basement for a moment of peace. Behind closed doors, she threw her hands up and said, "Thank you, Lord."

Grateful to diffuse the situation, she planned to make sure it never happens again. By the following Sunday, she had several projects she knew would keep them busy. No teen wanted to spend Saturdays cleaning a church. Michelle never had a problem with either of them again.

5

ZAHARA HUDSON

I n her feelings, Zahara had grown tired of her sister butting in her business. She was beyond upset that her sister pressed her to break up with Jacob, not understanding how attached the two were. It was easier said than done, India didn't seem to comprehend her sister's position in the matter. Being in a relationship with someone for almost three years was like being connected at the heart.

Zahara appreciated her sister's concern, but it drove her crazy at times. Sisterhood for the two of them meant being in each other's business, but some stuff she wanted to keep personal. The argument bothered her, and she didn't want to believe her sister's words. There was no way she was pregnant. She made the run to the store for a few items. Among the items on her grocery list were two pregnancy tests. She noticed a few changes in her body, which warranted a second opinion.

Anxious Zahara's trip to the store brought about all types of thoughts and flashbacks to her childhood. She never wanted her child to grow up in that manner. When she returned home, she drank a little cranberry juice and prepped dinner. Thankful to her bladder, she relieved herself and said a prayer for the best; who knew peeing on a stick could be such an important task. Not ready to know the results, she washed her hands and went back to the kitchen to tend to food.

Three months pregnant, Zahara weighed all her options before she did anything drastic. It was a shock, knocked up with by a married man was never part of her plan. The good part about her situation was how Jacob reacted to the news. She knew revealing being with child would force him to make things work. Neither was ready for the life-changing responsibility.

During alone time she did some soul searching and thought about the things her sister mentioned about getting serious. It was a life growing inside her stomach, a life she was responsible to provide for and love. Over the initial shock, the two discussed what life would consist of with a child added to the equation. Jacob had been thinking about Zahara's options for employment as well. Of course, it caused a tiff between them.

"Maybe we should find someone to fill in for you at the studio. It would allow time to breathe and figure out what you want to do."

"I like working because it keeps me busy, but eventually, yes I plan to work for a few more months, so please don't try to change my mind. Don't you like working with me?"

"It will be helpful because I would be able to focus better on the show. Having the mother of my child around who can become hormonally unbalanced at any time wouldn't look too hot," he confessed.

With a side eye, Zahara raised her eyebrow not sure to take his comment offensively or not. She shrugged it off as nothing when he reached for her feet offering a foot rub to relax her a bit. Zahara loved how Jacob tended to her needs, but she remained nervous about what the future held for them. Living the life she did with a married man had her in serious thought about things, and it scared her to know she'd push out a baby within a matter of time. She temporarily turned off her thinking cap and enjoyed the foot rub.

6

MICHELLE THOMAS

Michelle noticed Jacob's behavior had slightly changed, and it bothered her a great deal. He kept that darn iPhone X glued to his hand, showered more, and gave mixed signals to name a few. All were a sign that something wasn't right, but she had no time to worry about him. She had to put all of her attention to the sermon for Sunday.

Marriage hadn't been easy for the two of them lately because of the hectic schedule they shared. Jacob was one of the highest paid Christian hosts in the region. He served as a counselor in between television once a month. There once perfect marriage was in trouble on so many levels, but neither of them knew how badly

Unable to sleep through the night, Michelle stood and gazed out the window. It amazed her to see the snowfall given it was mid-April. It had to be close to five in the morning as she watched the snowflakes fall at a steady pace. She had recently packed all her winter clothing and boots. It appeared mother nature suffered from bipolar as it went from sixty-degree weather to a winter advisory all within a week. Michelle couldn't stop thinking about Deacon Jones and his words all the while stayed posted like a mannequin.

Shortly afterwards, she climbed down the stairs to the kitchen.

Michelle hit the light and moved towards the Keurig machine. She popped a Dunkin Donut k-cup inside, filled it with water, placing her favorite green Starbucks mug on the drip tray. The aroma of freshly brewed coffee filled her nostrils prompting her to take a deep breath in. It was something about the roasted coffee fragrance that perked her up with bits of energy. Once the cup had been filled to the rim, she added French vanilla creamer and two and a half spoonful's of sugar.

Carefully Michelle held the mug as she walked over to take a seat at the table. In a silent house, she could literally hear her own thoughts, some of which shouldn't be inside of a pastor's head. Deacon Jones never appeared to be attractive nor did she look at him in that way until recently. She assumed her feelings were a direct result from marriage issues and the idea that a man confessed to wanting her.

Several hours went by before Jacob made his way into bed, and yet again, he didn't bother to touch her. Awake, she laid there wondering what she did to drive him away. If anything, it left her confused. The roses and card indicated his affection yet there was no physical affection. In no mood to cause riff-raff, Michelle just laid in the dark until sleep found its way to her.

The next morning Michelle woke up with a stomach issue prompting her to run to the bathroom. Unsure if she ate something bad from Sunday's lunch or a bug caught her, she stayed home in bed. The body had a strange way of letting one know when enough was enough. Michelle was the type of person who kept busy all the time. She never knew when to take a break. It was safe to say her stomach situation was the only way to make her sit still.

Jacob climbed out of bed to check on her in an effort to show he cared about her well-being. While she hugged the toilet, he went to the kitchen to gather saltine crackers and something clear to drink. He put the items on a wooden serving tray and made his way back to the room. By then she had a cold face towel folded across her fore-head. Within thirty minutes, she was better, giving Jacob an excuse to shower, dress, and leave.

In an upright position, she had the perfect view of the outside from the high sitting queen sized bed. Big snowflakes fell from the sky in slow motion like a shaken snow globe. The weather had changed from all four seasons within a matter of two weeks. Michelle prayed she hadn't contacted anyone with the flu. TMJ4 news recently reported the flu this season had been the deadliest. Well enough to send a few emails, Michelle managed to retrieve her iPad to do a little work from home.

IMPROVED HEALTH BY MORNING, Michelle went to the church and didn't get home close to nine o'clock at night. Out of habit she parked in the garage then touched the hood of Jacob's car on the way past it. The cool feeling was a sign he'd been home for a while. She hit the button on the wall to let the garage door down. Quietly, she walked through the door that leads to the basement. Up five carpeted stairs, Michelle walked through the kitchen, which had a staircase leading to the second floor.

Sound asleep Jacob laid not moving one bit as she maneuvered around their room. She took a quick shower and changed into night-wear comfortable enough to keep her cool. Slowly she climbed in the bed next to Jacob hoping that he would reach over to touch any part of her body. Once he didn't, she took matters into her own hands by initiating contact. She slid closer to him, and with a few sensual strokes, the once soft piece of him grew hard. Glad she was still able to touch him the right way Michelle did something out of her normal behavior.

"Ahh, what are you doing, Michelle? I need sleep, baby. Don't do this to me." His words were the opposite of his actions, unable to resist her. Eager she raised her gown for Jacob to have easy access.

When he shifted and positioned himself on his back, he exposed himself. Unable to control herself, Michelle took what she wanted from a half-sleep Jacob. She climbed on top of him. Flushed with urges, the buildup of not making love for months turned her into a different person. During taking advantage of the opportunity, Jacob swiftly woke up to find her straddling him.

"What in the—" he tried to say, but the feeling of his wife rocking back and forth silenced him. He grabbed her close to him and finished the job she started, giving her the orgasm that she desperately needed.

Afterwards she slid from on top of him and swiftly headed to the bathroom. She took care of her hygiene and slivered back into bed satisfied. Michelle felt guilty for how she had just behaved. She took full advantage of Jacob. Although shameful that it had come down to taking sex from her husband, Michelle's urge had been fulfilled.

When Jacob removed himself from the bed, she remained still as if she had been sleeping. Once she heard the bathroom door close, she began to blink as continued to lie in the darkness. She glanced at the digital clock, which read *3:32 A.M.* and let out a loud sigh of frustration not able to fall asleep. That's when Jacob emerged from the bathroom and proceeded to get ready.

Michelle listened to his movement hesitant to speak up on the distance between them lately. She didn't want to start a fight or get upset, so she kept quiet and closed her eyes instead. Eventually, she dozed off, and Jacob left without so much as a goodbye. A bit naive Michelle had on blinders when it came to her husband, the love of her life. The notion of him cheating never crossed her mind regardless of the minor signs. Love is blind tended to be a true saying for the pastor who had troubles.

7

JACOB THOMAS

J acob woke up close to three A.M. and felt conflicted with the idea that his wife had physically taken sex from him. Typically, it wouldn't have bothered him, but this time around it made him feel dirty. Able to slide out the bed without disturbing Michelle, he stood and watched her sleep peacefully. Beautiful as she was the first time he laid eyes on her, Jacob wondered why he treated her so cold. He proceeded to the restroom for a steamy shower and then the closet to dress. In the process of preparing for work, he reflected on his rocky relationship. Being married to a pastor was difficult because the church always seemed to come first and Jacob second.

As a man of the cloth too, he understood the demand and tried to be patient. However, as a man, his patience wore thin, and his needs had begun to get neglected. Faithful for as long he could, Jacob found attention from another woman. Torn between two women, Jacob continued to wine and dine Michelle with flowers, cards, and gifts. On the other end, he spent any chance he could fornicating with Zahara.

Sadly, he had grown less attracted to his wife and sinfully more with her only because he felt entitled. He blamed his wife for his cheating because she never made him a priority. He blamed Zahara too. She was a seductress and had won his heart over the years. Unsure how much longer he could keep up the charade, living with two women at the same time had begun to take a toll on him.

Still dark outside, he left the house without telling Michelle good-bye. Jacob climbed inside his Benz and made the half an hour drive to the studio. He whipped into the parking garage and walked the short distance to the building. Not completely awake yet, he needed something to give him a boost. Not even in his office long enough for his computer to boot up, he was greeted by his assistant.

"Good morning, Mr. Thomas. Here is your coffee, cream, and four sugars," the female voice said.

He lifted his head to see a silhouette of the woman he had been with less than twenty-four hours ago. Zahara stood with a green Star-bucks coffee mug in hand and wore a smile that contagiously spread to him.

"Hi Ms. Hudson, thank you! You must have been reading my mind." He gently received the cup and took a sip of the warm liquid goodness. "Umm, just how I like it," he said with a wink.

"You have thirty minutes of peace before go time. Can I get you anything else?"

"As a matter of fact, there is something. Close the door for a second and come closer to me."

Zahara did as told and then seductively moved towards him as he sat at the edge of his desk. She wore a black V-neck, short sleeve, side zipper dress that flowed freely at the end. So freely he was able to slip his hand under it with easy access to her goodies.

"Let me touch that sweet thang before someone comes looking for us," he said and licked his lips. "I couldn't stop thinking about you last night."

"Oh yeah!" Zahara let out a quiet moan as something told her to regroup and stop him. His fingers felt so good that she hated they were at work. "No, we have to stop, baby. We cannot afford to get caught."

"If you say so," he replied, removing his hand from under her dress. He moved into the closet-sized half bathroom to wash his hands.

Jacob noticed Zahara had grabbed his coffee mug and took a few sips before she handed it to him. He drank from it surprised at how warm it still had been.

A quick glance at her wrist prompted him to do the same as they realized time had slipped by. They quickly exited his office and did a speed walk to the studio within a time record of six minutes. By the time Jacob took a seat and had his makeup applied, the cameraman made a signal. The topic of the morning revolved around temptation and staying true one's faith. Jacob was the last person to give advice because he didn't know the meaning of avoiding temptation. Nevertheless, none of the viewers knew his business, besides all men fall short.

"It's show time everyone! Get into position. Let's have a good show and keep those ratings up," Jacob announced, giving the crew a pep talk.

When the camera turned on, he didn't miss a beat for the next hour. When the camera got turned off, it was routine for the team to gather for comments and feedback for the taping. CNT along with a few other networks always shared the same building, so the place remained busy. Not obligated to stay the entire day, Jacob tended to spend no more than five hours there. The rest of his time was split between Zahara, counseling, and home to sleep.

By the late afternoon, Jacob and Zahara were able to finish what they started. While Zahara laid in Jacob's arms, she stroked his chest as their breathing calmed down to slow breaths. She made him feel like a man. He felt wanted again and attractive sexually. His affair had gone on so long that he no longer felt those guilty feelings. It was sad to say but cheating had become a normal part of his daily life. Ten years younger, Zahara made Jacob feel fresh and up to date. Their relationship began as emotional infidelity turned physical within a twelve-month span. Years later, Jacob continued to live two lives, toying with the hearts of two women.

Jacob extended his arm and grabbed his cell phone to check the time. The last thing he wanted to do was give Michelle something to complain about. He still felt weird from what happened earlier that morning between them. Nevertheless, he had to go home, which meant climbing out of bed with his hot piece of tail. He knew there was no way to get out of speaking to his wife.

"I really wish you didn't have to leave," Zahara said as she sat propped up on her left elbow.

"Yeah, me too," he dryly replied as he slipped on his black slacks and white-collar shirt.

"It's a shame there is only twenty-four hours in a day. We need more personal time together. We work together every day, and although the cat and mouse game is fun, I need more."

"Come on, baby. We've talked about this before. Give me a little more time. You know my situation." He moved closer and sat on the bed facing her.

"I'm not getting any younger nor do I want to be your little secret forever. Something's gotta give, Jacob."

"Divorce is not an option right now, point blank," he stated clearly in a tone that Zahara knew better to challenge. "My wife doesn't deserve what is happening now so imagine a divorce."

"I get it! Forget I even said anything," Zahara mumbled. She had an attitude written all over her face.

"Stop frowning. It doesn't fit you, honey. We both know I must go so don't make it harder. Now come give me a kiss to send me off," Jacob ordered.

She climbed on top of him and proceeded to give sensual pecks on the lips. One thing led to another, and as you can imagine, they went another round in the sheets.

8

MICHELLE THOMAS

Present Day

Michelle sat at her rich cherry wooden drop desk with the yellow legal pad in front of her. The black paper mate pen glided across the paper. She was on her second draft of the sermon. Something just didn't feel right prompting her to start over repeatedly. She realized it was time to take a break in an effort to relax her mind. She slid the chair from the desk and proceeded to lock up the office. Suddenly a bright idea came over her. Jacob texted midday to inform her he'd be busy taping and wouldn't make dinner.

To show effort, she made Jacob three meaty stuffed green peppers filled with ground beef with oozing cheesy, a crisp salad, and a little note in a small white envelope. Michelle wanted to work out the differences between the two of them because she genuinely loved him with all her heart. Wednesday evening, it was close to sixty degrees, and Michelle was dressed in a cute yet professional clergy dress. With the plate of food covered, she headed for her car ready to surprise her husband.

T.D. Jakes' Podcast played through the speakers of her Lexus truck while she drove to the studio. A forty-five-minute drive gave Michelle time to reflect on the words she planned to tell Jacob. As a wife, she had neglected him but planned to do better with baby steps. First with surprise dinners, then oral sex, and lastly something so spontaneous he'd never forget. Michelle pulled into the parking garage of CNT Studios and found a spot by the door. She hit the push start button and shut the car off, got out, and retrieved the plate careful not to drop it.

Usually, an uncomfortable eerie feeling passed through her body whenever she felt something wrong. Michelle entered with a smile, but her pleasant demeanor disappeared when she walked in on Jacob with another woman. She didn't know what was worse, catching him in the act or finding out he lied. Beyond devastated the betrayal hurt worst which caused her to lash out.

A stare down between the two became so intense that Michelle had called him every name in the book with her eyes. Michelle stormed out not giving Jacob enough time to catch up to her. In the car, she drove off in a hurry as she cried the entire drive. She did her best not to speed or run any red lights along the way.

FINALLY, home and unable to think clearly, Michelle grabbed a bottle of Crane Lake Sweet Red, not bothering to grab a glass. She removed the black rubber wine stopper and took a few swigs to the head like a wino on the corner. Then suddenly it hit her, Angela Bassett from the movie *Waiting to Exhale* gave her an idea. No longer functioning like a woman of the cloth, Michelle marched upstairs and right into the walk-in closet. Hands on hip, she stood and glanced over all his expensive Italian suits and designer shoes with an evil grin.

The devil had convinced her to do things that she normally wouldn't have done, but when love was a part of the picture, people did crazy things. Michelle selected the items she knew Jacob loved the most. In a subtle manner, she took the bag downstairs with her outside on the patio. She scattered some of the items in the fire pit, not hesitating to pour lighter fluid, then lit and tossed a match. The fire slowly burned, and it soothed the anger from her body as she watched the flames danced.

So focused on the burning flames, she hadn't realized Jacob made it home until the sound of his voice alerted her. Without so much as a head turn, she never acknowledged him as he cussed and fussed about his stuff burning. His reaction put a smirk on Michelle's face. She was glad to see him hurt. After he stormed out, she burned more stuff before going back inside. Michelle spent the rest of the evening lounging around the house until she dozed off.

THE NEXT MORNING, the sun rays shined through the white blinds right into Michelle's eyes, causing her to squint. She laid in bed with a slight hangover as she tried to forget the actions of last night's event. The mobile phone rang causing her to let out a deep sigh before she answered.

"Good morning, this is pastor," she answered doing her best to sound wide-awake. The voice on the other end was her personal assistant, Tracy, a young woman who grew up attending Temple Faith.

"Sorry to phone so early but you told me to call if Bishop James got in touch. His secretary sent an email confirmation ten minutes ago. I also have the first draft of your sermon printed and on your desk."

"That is wonderful news, Tracy. I'll be there in the next two hours. I'm getting a late start this morning."

"No problem, Pastor. I'll hold things down until you arrive. You deserve to drag your feet every once in a while," Tracy convinced Michelle.

"You're right! Thank you again for the update. See ya in a bit," Michelle commented, ending the call.

She climbed out the bed letting out a yawn as she slipped her feet inside the cozy, black slippers. Once she enjoyed a cup of coffee and two bagels with strawberry cream cheese, her body began to wake up. Back upstairs, she showered and slipped into a black tapered dress. After Michelle finished getting dressed and packed her bag, she headed out to the garage ready for a peaceful drive to the church.

The parking lot was empty as Michelle pulled into a space. She knew the quiet would only last a few hours. On Thursdays and Saturdays, the praise dance girls practiced along with the choir and drummers. Michelle loved to take a break to sneak and listen. She made her way into the building, and she felt nine times better than before. When she walked into the house of the Lord, all her troubles rolled away, giving her a free reign to help others. Whenever she spent time at the church, it made her forget her personal problems. The second she turned the corner nearby her office, her assistant whose back was faced towards her greeted her.

Tracy spoke out, "Good morning, Pastor."

"Impressive. How did you know it was me?" Michelle asked.

"The sound of your heels makes a little pitter patter click to it. That is one of those things I've learned over time listening to everyone walk back and forth all day," Tracy confessed.

"Interesting. Well, I'm going to check my emails, review the sermon you left for me, and a few other miscellaneous things. Please hold calls unless it's super important."

"Okie dokie," Tracy replied. She continued to do filing as Michelle sashed into her office and softly shut the door.

Michelle wasted no time getting started on the many tasks that awaited her attention. Once her computer booted up, she pulled up Pandora, and for ten minutes straight, she sifted through emails keeping the important ones marked unread. Next, she cleared a space in front of her and laid out her big bible and the edited sermon. Tracy always made sure to attach a small color sticky note where my attention was needed. The red pen markings were edited punctuation and sentence structure. Within an hour, she managed to complete her new draft with a few additions. Afterwards she made a few calls to some of the neighboring churches, which passed time.

Knock! Knock!

Unsure why Tracy didn't buzz her first, Michelle stood from her chair and moved from behind the desk. She personally opened the door to find Erica, the choir director and church pianist. Erica had been the pianist for over ten faithful years.

"Hi, Sister Erica! How you are doing on this blessed day?"

"I won't complain, Pastor. The girls are about to run through their routine for Sunday. They've been practicing their little hearts out."

"I actually was about to chat with Tracy about my sermon, and then I'll make my way to the sanctuary," Michelle assured Erica.

Michelle did just that and then walked the short distance to the double doors. Upon entering the sanctuary, Erica played Yolanda Adams' "The Battle Is The Lord's" on the piano. Quietly she slid inside a pew and watched from afar. Dancing and praising the Lord at a young age impressed the pastor. As she observed the young ladies, it warmed her heart to see them give praise and spend time inside a church versus the streets. Baby fever had kicked into full effect even though she could not bear a child. Once the dance ended, Michelle clapped and rose from her seat and strolled towards the front of the church.

"Ladies you did a terrific job! I'm sure everyone will enjoy it as much as I did," she assured.

"Okay ladies let's get changed and then we can stop for lunch," Erica insisted.

"YEESSSS!" the girls exclaimed and ran to the back room.

"Food is always an incentive to get them excited," Erica commented.

"Sure is," Michelle agreed and let out a chuckle. "Well, let me get downstairs so that I can finish up and grab a bit myself. Enjoy your day."

∼

LATE AFTERNOON her sermon had been finalized and titled "We All Fall Short of God's Glory". Jacob had inspired her words of wisdom she planned to preach on Sunday. With no one at home waiting for her, Michelle gathered her belongings, turned out the light, and headed out of the office. Tracy had already left for the day prior to leaving detailed notes for Michelle.

9

JACOB THOMAS

J acob grew mentally and physically drained overtime as his moral conscious began to get the best of him. He tried to keep up an appearance for those who weren't aware of his side affair. Zahara's news about a love child on the way added stress on him. There was no one to blame for the mistakes made but the man who created them, and now he had to man up. Jacob didn't believe in abortions and always wanted a child of his own. Therefore, the unexpected news from Zahara put him in a difficult situation. One that could end his marriage for good.

As he laid in bed unable to sleep, every solution he tried to come up with involved keeping the baby and coming clean to Michelle. Although they hardly expressed it, their love for one another were deep like tree roots in the ground.

With every fiber and bean in his body, he still loved and wanted things to work out with his wife. Becoming a father was a long time coming, only now it was with the wrong woman. He continued to toss and turn until his alarm went off at three-thirty in the morning. With an open hand, Jacob hit the snooze button and turned over as sleep had finally come to him. Suddenly, he hopped up and realized he had less than an hour to shower, eat, and get to work.

BARELY ON TIME to the television studio, had Jacob's personal life began to affect his ability to focus at work? Sips of coffee helped wake him up as he went over the script. The show's guest waited backstage until it was time for them to appear on screen. In a swift moment George, the camera operator, alerted Jacob they would go live in less than three minutes. Jacob cleared his throat and took another sip of coffee.

The studio was set up like a typical interview layout with two armchairs on each side of the stage. A tall, plastic plant sat in the corners of the room. The backdrop behind the chairs consisted of the CNT Network letters. It was a cozy looking set-up.

"Okay, it's show time crew get ready. Five. Four. Three. Two. One." When George's finger pointed to Jacob, he came in right on cue.

"Good morning! This is Jacob, and you're tuned into Christian Network Television. Today our special guest is Bishop James, Welcome!"

"It's a pleasure," Bishop replied then flashed a smile.

"Let's jump right in. Your book releases today in all major bookstores. How are you feeling?"

"Nervous but most importantly, I'm blessed. It's hard to believe this is my sixth book. Each release feels like the first time."

"Now I'm sure those watching have a burning question for you. Where did the inspiration come from for this project?" Jacob slightly turned his body in the bishop's direction ready for the scoop.

"I won't speak for other authors, but usually, my ideas come from a combination of life, people watching, and music. Certain music triggers memories that translate into a story."

Directly after the show, Tyler summoned Jacob and his team to the meeting lounge. He had updates and comments on their overall performance for the past three months. Once everyone took a seat, Tyler stood in front of the room ready to address them. He praised everyone on a great job before he moved into the important matters.

"Jacob, do you mind hanging back for a minute?" Tyler asked just as he was about to rise up from his chair. The others made their exit and then Tyler closed the door and took a seat.

"Am I in some kind of trouble?" Jacob asked in a serious tone.

"I wanted to tell you how well the ratings have been and some feedback to keep the numbers going up. As you know, Southeastern Regional Pastor Wallace and his wife will be guests in less than a week. Everything must be perfect, including you."

Jacob let out a sigh of relief when he thought Tyler was finished, but he continued.

"I know about the mishaps with your assistant and wife. That can never happen again, or you are out of here. No drama at work," he stressed.

"I understand. Thank you for the warning, and you don't have to worry about that situation anymore. My personal life will stay just that, personal," Jacob promised.

~

IT DIDN'T SEEM as if Jacob had been at CNT Studios for three years already. The television crew along with the producers decided to surprise him with a marble sheep cake to celebrate. A good ten folks gathered in a semicircle with Jacob in the middle as Zahara used a plastic cake cutter. She placed square medium sized pieces of cake on Dixie heavyweight paper plates.

"It has been a great pleasure to have you around, Jacob. you've helped turn CNT into a top viewing syndicate. Thank you for being a great team member and member of the family!" Tyler stated.

"Wow!" Jacob was taken aback by the surprise party. "This is very cool, thank you all a bunch. Time has gone by so fast. It is hard to believe I have been here that long. Working with all of you have been rewarding and challenging. However, we have grown close like a family and I'm grateful."

~

ZAHARA'S HORMONES made her crazier than she was before she got pregnant. Her actions kept him walking on eggshells because she kept threatening to tell his wife about the baby. Anything he did that she didn't like, she would use the baby as a threat. Stuck in a difficult situation, he couldn't take the threats anymore. Jacob decided to get together with Michelle to reveal the secret. He figured he owed her that much. In addition, he didn't want her to find out from another woman.

Jacob tried to find the best way to reveal the news to Michelle about the pregnancy. Honestly, he knew there was never a good way to reveal this type of news to an already angry, black woman. He witnessed her burn clothes, so she was capable of doing worse if tempted. In need of advice, he never really had a core person to confide in, so he did the next best thing. He prayed on it and did what he felt was best, which was to come clean to his wife.

A DAY later Michelle surprisingly accepted his invite to lunch so that he could reveal his secret. Jacob figured they could reconcile for the sake of their marriage and image. However, he came prepared for things to go left during the lunch.

"Well I asked you here today because there is something you need to know, and it should come from me. I understand this is a sensitive topic, but I must tell you. Umm, Zahara is expecting."

"Expecting what?" The second she registered his words he didn't have to say anything further. "A baby? Really Jacob, how could you?" The hurt in her face and voice was deja vu all over again.

"Chelle, I'm so sorry. This wasn't supposed to happen. She has been threatening to tell you whenever she gets mad, so I took the liberty to confess."

"Let me get this straight. You cheat, make a baby, and move out and leave me looking stupid. Who does that to the woman who has been loyal and faithful since day one? A selfish ungrateful sorry excuse for a man."

She got quiet when the server approached, not even in the mood to eat anything. Though the moment was ruined, she still had some stuff to say before she stormed away.

"What have you done to our marriage, Jacob? Can you imagine how people will look at me on Sunday mornings if this news gets out?" she asked and shook her head.

"Chelle, we're both to blame in this, and you know it," he shot back as he tried to keep his voice down.

"Oh yeah, that's real typical of you to blame me for your screwing around and making a baby. As your partner, you should've told me you were unhappy."

"How?" he said quickly. "You're never home, and when you are, church still consumes you. That is the reason I found comfort in Zahara."

To avoid losing her tongue, she politely removed herself from the table, walked away without a word to Jacob She never looked back.

In that moment, he felt weight lifted off his shoulders, however, the battle between two women only meant more drama down the line. Zahara had his heart and baby while Michelle was his backbone and mate. In a tangled web of trouble, Jacob ate the food that nourished his body and gave him strength to go deal with a hormonal mistress.

10

MICHELLE THOMAS

Once Jacob revealed that Zahara was pregnant with his child, Michelle wanted to call him every name but son of God. The anger fumed in her like it did when she burned his clothes. She wanted to toss her glass of water in his face. Beyond upset, she held her tongue and remained calm a little longer. News about a baby was the last thing she expected to hear about. The more Michelle tried to wrap her head around the news, the angrier she became. Her foot shook so fast underneath the table that her leg had gone into autopilot.

Unable to have children made the news Jacob delivered even more painful to bear. There were years of trying only to be disappointed in the end. Michelle found herself at times questioning why the Lord blessed some with children and not others. There were countless news stories about parents who abused and even killed kids. She never understood how monsters like that were given such a precious gift.

The more things unfolded in her marriage, Michelle grew thankful that she and Jacob didn't have children. The drama would have intensified. She came to more of a realization that the one thing she wanted just wasn't meant for her. Although the pain deepened, she tried not to dwell. After all, it wasn't nothing a good workout, prayer, and glass of wine couldn't handle.

FOR THREE WEEKS, Michelle enjoyed her serenity with Jacob out of the house. It gave her time to reflect and face the issues head-on. However, her peace was short lived by a surprise visit. The unexpected sound of the doorbell woke her from a good sleep drawing her from the warm queen-sized bed. In slow motion, she made her way down each wooden stair. Michelle finally had a chance to sleep in, then the freaking doorbell.

"Just a second!" she yelled as she approached the arch-topped mahogany door. The face on the other side was her brother. "Nick?" Unrecognizable his body parts had changed, but she held her tongue.

"Surprise! It's me, sis! Please call me Nikki. It's my new name. May I enter?"

"Oh yes, sorry," Michelle apologized as she moved to the side still in denial.

To say it was the wrong time for him to visit would be an understatement. Nick had a bad habit of sticking his nose where it didn't belong. When confronted he had the nerve to throw scriptures at Michelle. Estranged from each other for a few years, she wondered how long the visit would last.

"So, what brings you this way after so long? Not that I'm not happy to see you," she clarified her statement.

"Well, I'm in town for a possible gig, and I figured I should stop by. I'll probably stay for three days before flying back to North Carolina."

"Oh okay, that's cool. Well, it's nice to see you even though you look completely different. If you don't mind me asking, are you fully transitioned now?"

"Let's just say, I can officially shop for bra and panties, just like all the other women. I'm comfortable in my skin, and I pray that you can do the same. This transition means the world to me."

"I just don't understand. How do you know this is the best choice to make?" Michelle had always been curious but never had the nerve to ask details.

"Imagine living a lie most of your life to please others while you felt miserable. It's my life and choice. Remember when we played dress up, that is how I knew. It's something I can't explain sis."

"I'm not one to judge, and I accept and love you no matter what. You should know that by now. Regardless of my beliefs, we are blood, and that matters more to me. Aye, let's go to the kitchen."

"How is Jacob doing? Is he still a preacher man too?"

"He is fine, and no, he stepped down from the pulpit to do more counseling." She wanted to reveal that he was a no-good cheating dog like all men, but she kept that dirt to herself.

Unable to lie, she only told part of the story to avoid more questions and to save herself from embarrassment. Michelle had always been the perfect one who had everything in life. As the older sibling, she tried to set an example, but even she dealt with drama.

"Help yourself to whatever is in the fridge or cabinets. I haven't been to the store yet. I'll go tomorrow after church. If you need something, make a list."

"Dang sis, where is your refrigerator? All I see are cabinets," Nikki inquired.

"Girl, it's a built-in fridge," Michelle stated. She then opened the ivory color French doors. "The dishwasher is the same way."

"Damn, that's niiice! You fancy as heck, sista," Nikki joked.

Still hung up on the fact that her brother was now her sister, it took Michelle some time to adjust the new transformation. If their parents were still alive, she knew they would've disowned him for his choice.

"Dang sis, you got tons of fruits, vegetables, and bougie water, but where is the meat at?"

"First off what is bougie water?" Michelle asked then chuckled.

"Fiji water. That's expensive, girl," Nikki joked.

During them joking, Michelle's phone rang, and she excused herself from the room. It was Saturday and close to noon. She had no plans on leaving the house, but Tracy's call changed her plans, yet again. By the time she strolled back to the kitchen, the smell of turkey sausage frying hit her nose.

"What you are hooking up in here, sista chef?"

"Turkey sausage and pasta, nothing too spectacular. Who was that one the phone?"

"Hey nosey," Michelle shot back in a funny manner. "It was the church, and I've been summoned, but I'm not leaving until I eat a bowl of that pasta."

Given some of her brother's (now sister) life choices, the two hadn't always seen eye to eye. Nevertheless, she loved him. Opposite in lifestyles, Michelle believed in the bible and the notion that man and woman belonged together. Their parents never understood his true journey of 'finding the true him' as he called it. In a transition phase, Nick wanted to become Nikki, and that was one of those choices Michelle had a hard time accepting it. The idea bounced in her head like the dice in the plastic bubble of a Trouble game.

LATER THAT NIGHT the two continued their bonding time over dinner like any other set of siblings. In a way, it relieved Michelle to have company in the house because she grew lonely, yet it also gave her another chance to get close with Nikki. After all, she had to practice what she preached, which was love those who ever so need it, and treat those you meet like family.

"I finally feel free to be me, the person I'm destined to be regardless of the chatter. No one would ever comprehend the agony, the wear, and tear, and pressure one faces in a cruel world like we live in. Being born different used to scare me but not now! Nope."

Michelle had no idea her brother felt that way as he made the decision to become a woman.

ALTHOUGH MICHELLE LOVED the visit from her sister, of course, Nikki had overstayed her welcome. She had items strolled throughout the house, shoes in every room and other pet peeve turn-offs. A neat freak, Michelle loved her home clean and hated to see things out of place.

Practically two weeks later, enough had been enough, Michelle braved the nerves to speak with Nikki over dinner. Unsure of the outcome of their conversation, it was something that had to be done. She took a deep breath in then exhaled before speaking.

"Sis, you know I love you, and I pray that my words don't offend you, but it's about that time. It's been nice catching up and reminiscing, but Jacob will be coming back home soon." Michelle felt bad lying to Nikki but figured that was the easiest way to get her out.

"Chelle, honey, I know when I'm not wanted, but thank you for trying to be nice about it. I'll be gone in the morning. You got my word."

"Nikki, I-" Michelle attempted to speak, but Nikki held up her hand.

"For what it's worth, you don't have to front or lie about Jacob. It's okay not to be perfect all the time. From the time I got here, I've watched you. You're not the same happy-go- lucky sister."

"I'm just tired that's all. I'm still the same sister. Thanks for your concern."

"And Jacob?"

"We had a disagreement like all married folks do. It's nothing to worry about, I promise. Well, I'm gonna call it a night. I've got an early start in the morning. Love you, sis," Michelle whispered.

"Love ya back!"

Michelle headed up the stairs and couldn't help but think about what Nikki had said. Things hadn't been the same, and she feared it wouldn't get better. That was one reason she kept her personal trials secret. Nikki had all the advice in the world for others but not herself.

11

ZAHARA HUDSON

Since Jacob confessed to Michelle, Zahara had to figure out her next move. She gave Jacob an ultimatum. It was divorce or eighteen years of hell, his choice. She felt so stupid, but the deed had been done, a baby would be born who needed a mother. Without a father figure, she was determined not to repeat the cycle for their child. Home alone, Zahara used the time to snack on fruits and read baby books. In bed, she adored the pregnancy pillow that Jacob ordered for her. It was a godsend, as she was able to lay and sleep comfortably. Down for a nap, she dozed off within a matter of minutes.

LATER THAT EVENING Jacob came over to check on her, but she gave him the silent treatment. His living a double life seemed fun to him, but for her it was fudged up. Knocked up without a secure plan wasn't cool at all. She could hear India's voice in her head to leave Jacob alone, but Zahara's heart wouldn't allow her. Firm in her decision not to give in, she refused to have sex with him. That was until he stepped out the shower half-naked with nothing but the towel wrapped around his waist.

"Oh my," she said not realizing he heard her, giving him a reason to turn and speak.

"Like what you see, huh? I knew you couldn't stay mad at me forever," he joked as he made his pecs jump. "How are you feeling?" His concern for her made the anger turn into sexual attraction. The hormones took over, and she found herself snatching the towel from his waist as he stood exposed.

AT SIX MONTHS ALONG, Zahara laid back in bed with a hand on her stomach. It was still surreal that a little human being was growing inside of her. Tired, she rested her head back on the Supima cotton pillowcase. As her eyes remained closed, material that she had been reading swirled through her mind while she drifted off for a nap. While asleep, she dreamed she had a pregnancy complication after giving birth. The dream seemed so real that Zahara quickly jumped up while holding her stomach.

Zahara: Jacob it's imperative we have to talk when you get home. I had a crazy dream that freaked me out. Hope your day is going well!

JT: I'll be there as soon as I can, dear! It may be another a few hours. Do you want me to pick up anything?

Zahara: Ok. Nothing specific now. I'll text if I think of anything between now and later. See you soon.

Zahara sent the text and tossed the phone to the side of the bed in a rush to empty her bladder. By the time she finished and stepped out, Jacob had walked through the door headed towards the bedroom.

"Hey honey," he said.

"Jacob I've been thinking about something and please hear me out. It might sound strange, but here it goes. Do you think your wife is up to helping raise our child?" Zahara asked as she gently sat down on the bed.

Jacob almost choked on his iced tea as he coughed and cleared his throat. He wiped the tear from his eye and gave her his undivided attention, interested to hear her argument.

"In the event that something happens to me, I need to know my baby will be loved and cared for by you and my sister. That includes your wife if she doesn't leave your ass officially."

Jacob seemed surprised by Zahara's wish but admitted it made sense although he didn't understand why she had come to that conclusion. He thought before he spoke carefully not to say the wrong thing to create a hormonal scene.

"I pray it doesn't come to that, baby. We are going to raise our son together and give him all the love he'll need," he asserted and gripped her hand.

"You didn't answer the question. We did something awful, and I'm scared that my karma is around the corner ready to collect."

"Where is all of this coming from?" Jacob questioned. Taken aback from the entire conversation, he took a deep breath. "Deep down I think she will. Her love for a child has no bearing on our actions."

"Aye, we should I mean you should invite her to lunch in the next day or so to ask her. I mean being a pastor and all she supposed to forgive people, right. Like you said an innocent child deserves love."

"Woah, you are moving too fast, Z," Jacob interjected. Yes, she is a pastor, but she is also a woman nonetheless. We'd be lucky if she even agrees to meet, but I guess it's worth a try. I'll do my best to make it happen only if we change topics," he pleaded.

"Thank you," she said and leaned over to plaster a kiss on his cheek.

12

MICHELLE THOMAS

Michelle no longer held a grudge against Jacob or Zahara. It took too much energy from her. She also accepted Nikki. She prayed about the situation and took things one day at a time. Although her life was like a movie, she saved face, and her personal business remained confidential. The separation and pregnancy of Jacob's mistress had remained between the three of them, although there were times Michelle wished she could pour out her sorrows to someone.

Each day she gained a piece of herself back from being a broken woman in an effort to love again. Betrayal by a spouse hurt more than she cared to admit, but each tear she shed she wiped her eyes and kept going. The voice of the Lord told her to keep on going. There was life to live. Her hurting heart had started to heal again, and then she received a phone call from Jacob. Her finger quickly tapped the ignore button as she pondered his reason for calling her up. Seconds later the red voicemail symbol popped on, and Michelle clicked it to listen.

Hey Chelle,

I pray all is well your way! I'm probably the last person you want to

hear from, but there is some stuff we need to talk about ASAP. Please
consider meeting me at Elsa's on the Park around noon. It's imperative we
have a much-needed conversation. Text me back to let me know what you
decide. Have a blessed day.

    Jacob

AFTER SHE LISTENED to his message, a part of her was glad to hear his
husky voice. It took her back to the first time they talked on the
phone during their courting days. He called her every night before
bedtime just so he could be the man in her dreams. It was corny but
sweet, and she fell in love with him. That's the man she missed and
wanted back in her life, so naturally the softy in her texted him.

    PM: *Hi Jacob, all is well. I'm just being a servant to the Lord and*
praying for those in need. You know how busy my schedule is so please
don't have me show up for nothing. See you tomorrow. Chelle

AGAINST HER BETTER JUDGMENT, Michelle made the drive to Elsa's as a
part of her agreement with Jacob. Upon entering the restaurant,
Michelle noticed Jacob who stood to his feet and signaled. She
walked in his direction and noticed Zahara in a seat next to him,
which made her sick to the stomach. Seeing Zahara for the first time
since the incident suddenly took her back to the evening that she
caught them having sex in his office.

    She put on a fake smile the closer she grew to them, but it was
wiped away when Zahara stood up with an extended hand. Michelle
was taken aback at the size of her baby bump as she realized the
urgency of the sit-down. Being blindsided hurt, but seeing another
woman pregnant by her husband felt like a blow to the stomach.
Despite it all, she remained calm.

    "Hey guys," she greeted them dryly and took a seat declining to
shake Zahara's hand. Not wanting to appear as the bitter one,

Michelle kept all petty comments to herself. Instead, a smile crept across her face again, the fakest smile she had ever forced.

"Chelle thanks for agreeing to meet us. I'm sure this is an unpleasant situation, so I'll be quick. Since we'll be a blended family soon, I prayed we could chat like adults."

"You mean cheating on me and having a love child wasn't enough?" her sarcasm slipped out. Zahara sat without speaking one word.

"Really Chelle. I've apologized numerous times, and the past can't be changed. I called because Zahara and I want to know if you would be willing to help. You know it takes a village to raise a child."

"Jacob I cannot believe you! How dare you call me down here to ask something like that? If I wasn't saved," she muttered. Then she directed her attention in Zahara's direction.

"You. I hope you're pleased that you broke up a marriage. How does it feel to be a homewrecker? Y'all got me all messed up. I'm done with this foolishness," Michelle raged. Just as she was about to remove herself from the table, Zahara shot back.

"Actually, your marriage had been in trouble before I came in the picture. Jacob seems to be very happy now, especially with his first child on the way."

A lump formed in her throat as Zahara's words hit her hard like a punch to the throat. She even went as far to rub her stomach in a taunting manner. It almost killed Michelle, but she held it together long enough to make an exit. Drawn back into a sunken place, she drowned her sorrows in a bottle of Stella Rosa the second she made it home.

GLAD TO GET her mind off the marital drama, Michelle and Tracy made sure the fellowship hall had been perfectly decorated, and the food was on point. The partner church's Outreach Luncheon event between Destiny Temple and Temple Faith had to be perfect. Sister churches for a decade, Destiny Temple did two partnering events each month. They even provided lunch on Sundays, which fed over a hundred or more people. That was the same church Deacon Jones transferred to in efforts to avoid Michelle.

Michelle and Deacon Jones were forced to be around each other during the entire luncheon. The more they tried to avoid each other, the more they were brought face to face. Finally, they ended up by the beverage table, and the awkward silence prompted Michelle to speak first to keep them from looking weird.

"How has it been working out at our sister church?" She raised the plastic cup of lemonade to her mouth.

"It's okay. Everyone is friendly and very helpful. I won't lie. I miss this place but... you know," he said purposely not looking her in the eyes.

"We miss you too! I sure wish there was a way to work something out to get you back. So much has changed since your departure."

"Oh yeah, nothing that the Lord can't help mend I'm sure."

"I'm not so sure about that," she mumbled as she put the cup to her lips again.

"Come again," he said as he leaned his ear closer to hear her.

"Nothing. Umm, I should go back to the table and take a seat. You are coming?"

"I'm right behind you."

Deacon Jones let out a sigh as he followed behind the chocolate woman he so craved. The two sat across from one another giving them a perfect view of the forbidden. They turned their attention to the front of the room when Pastor Joe's voice pierced through the microphone. Michelle tried so hard to keep her attention focused up front but ended up daydreaming. The sound of everyone clapping their hands brought her back to reality.

The goal of the luncheon event focused on fellowship and exchanging ideas. Everyone mingled and talked about plans to increase more outreach to keep the kids off the streets. Both churches provided those needs but needed strategies on how to approach the kids. The luncheon turned out to be a success and only lasted three hours. Tracy helped with clean up left immediately after. Michelle trailed behind her by ten minutes as she walked to her car not expecting to see Deacon James.

"What are you doing here? Did you forget something?"

"Nope, I couldn't leave without saying something to you. No matter how I fight it, I end up right back here."

"Deacon Jones, I thought you-"

"Please call me David," he interjected as he closed the distance between them. No longer able to fight it he flat out asked her something that changed her whole understanding. "Earlier you said things changed since I left. What were you referring to exactly, personal or church?"

Quiet, Michelle couldn't believe how bold Deacon Jones had gotten within a matter of hours. After all, he had the problem with being around her, so the mixed signals confused the situation no less. Her attraction to him made her uncomfortable because she was vulnerable, especially after seeing Zahara's baby bump.

"I didn't mean anything by it. It's nothing to concern yourself with anyway."

During their conversation, they stood in the parking lot as if time had frozen and no one around them mattered. Somehow someway the devil found his way to them because out of nowhere, Deacon Jones leaned in and kissed Michelle on the lips. The kiss surprised them both, but neither of them pulled back. Instead, their lips locked longer than they should have.

"Oh, my goodness! I gotta go. I gotta go!" Michelle repeated, and she fumbled with her car keys.

She didn't give him time to say anything as he just stood there and watched her climb in the car. She started the engine, slipped on her seatbelt, and glanced at Deacon Jones before pulling off.

∾

Unable to get Deacon Jones or the kiss out of her head, Michelle couldn't help but think about the forbidden attraction the two shared. He transferred to another church because the temptation was too great. Never did she believe another man besides Jacob could've have made her feel that way. But now, she truly felt conflicted on what to do even though she knew the answer.

In the past, she never looked at another man because of the commitment and love for Jacob. Church duties occupied most of her time, not leaving room to partake in sinful acts. Fast forward to now, the rich, mocha man had been the cause of impure thoughts that filled Michelle's mind. Once she told him about her troubles at home, they finally let their guard down.

A week later, Michelle worked on a proposal to get more funding for the church. She had given Tracy strict instructions not to buzz her unless it was truly an emergency. While she reviewed the proposal for the third time, it made her realize how important a second set of eyes were. In need of a break, she removed her glasses from her face sitting them on her desk. Just as she leaned back in her chair, Tracy buzzed her.

"Yes Tracy," she answered.

"Pastor Deacon Jones is on the line for you. Should I take a message?"

"No!" she answered realizing how might have sounded. "Umm, I mean I'll speak with him. Thank you."

"Okay, he is on line one," Tracy said before clicking over.

"Pastor Michelle?" Deacon Jones spoke making Michelle close her eyes in awe of his voice.

"Yes! I'm here. How are you today, deacon?"

"Blessed and highly favored! I pray all is well your way. I um, called because I think we need to have a talk. I've prayed about it, and I really need to see you," he disclosed.

"Actually, I just finished reviewing the proposal and could use your feedback. Are you open for dinner later? You pick the place."

"Six o'clock at my place?" he asked.

Eyes widened by his response she tried to resist the feelings that had suddenly stirred up inside. "Um, sure, that will work if you think that's best. I just remember what happened last time."

"Yeah, I know, which is one of the reasons for this sit-down. I left the church to avoid you, but ever since I did, we find ourselves closer and closer. Let's finish this talk later. If you are allergic to anything, please text me at 414-255-6224."

"Okay. I will do that! Have a good rest of the day," she expressed.

"Same to you Michelle, bye."

Michelle hung up the phone speechless at what had just transpired between the two of them. Their last encounter resulted in them kissing which has been something she'd been thinking about constantly. At that moment, she wondered if Jacob felt the way she did when decided to sleep with Zahara. Either way, she had no intentions of crossing that line, yet she did want to kiss him again.

By three-thirty, Michelle made her way home to prepare for an unpredictable evening with a man who craved her just as much as she did him. Undecided on a clergy outfit or regular clothing, she kept telling herself to dress respectfully rather than a desperate woman. Finally, she decided on a knee length skirt, something neutral that didn't display her curves. In the body mirror, she admired herself when the phone sounded and diverted her attention. She moved to the bed and picked it up trying not to smile or show excitement.

DJ: Dinner will be done shortly. I assume you don't have any food allergies since you never sent a message. Please click on the link and it will lead you right to my doorsteps. Bring your appetite! http://goo.gl/maps/ydC8i7oh9Qt

Michelle clicked on the link and realized how close he lived which was a surprise to her. She never knew where he lived, and in all honesty, it probably turned out to be the best thing. Up until now, Michelle had avoided sin, and she prayed that she could control herself the evening.

PM: Got it! I never knew you lived twelve minutes away. See you shortly.

DJ: :-)

She took one last look at herself then grabbed a light jacket and pocketbook and headed down the stairs and straight to the garage. She climbed in her car and said a quick prayer before she backed out and drove to Deacon Jones' home.

13

ZAHARA HUDSON

June 2018

Zahara inhaled eight pieces of hot fried chicken wings with jalapeno peppers and water. Her cravings were nonstop as she continued to grow big as a house. Near the ending of her pregnancy, she had grown to love her son. The feeling of him growing and moving inside her was nothing short of a miracle. Stuffed liked a turkey she propped back on the sofa with her swollen feet up on a pillow. Home alone, her plan entailed a good book and snacks.

Cozy and comfortable Zahara got the urge to pee but refused to move. Apparently, she thought she had control over her bladder. Suddenly the feeling of a pop and wetness between her legs begged to differ. She slowly peeled her body from the sofa only to slip back down.

"AHH!" she yelled aloud trying not to panic as she placed her hand over her stomach. She grabbed her iPhone 8 and quickly called her sister.

"Come on, sis, pick up," she mumbled as the phone rang.

"Hey, sissy!"

"India! I need you to stop whatever you're doing and get over here. I think my water just broke. Please come as fast as you can. Use the key under the rug to let yourself in."

"WHAT! I'm on my way."

"Hurry!" Zahara yelled and hung up then called Jacob next. She didn't care where he was or who he was with. She needed him. The phone rang three almost four times before he finally answered.

"Hello. Zahara, I'm with a patient right now. Can this wait?"

"Jacob, the baby is coming. I need you. Please meet me and India at St. Luke's."

"The baby, what? Oh my god! Okay, I'm wrapping up right now. I'll meet you."

"Okay, please don't come too late. You have to witness the birth of your son!"

"Baby I won't miss the most precious moment of our lives. Love you." His words to her were so sincere.

Although she was not in pain, Zahara remained on the sofa scared to move as she silently vowed never to get pregnant again. The experience was one to remember, but the hard part hadn't started yet. She laid and debated on the use of epidural or natural childbirth. Unsure if she could withstand the pain without the shot, she had to decide sooner than later. Her thoughts were interrupted when her sister entered the door ready to transport her to the hospital.

"I'm here to save the day," India said as she stood in the doorway looking at Zahara.

"Sis, I'm so glad to see you girl! I tried to get up but fell back down. You gotta help me up, but first I need something."

"What?"

"Can I get a few yogurt covered raisins from the kitchen?"

"Dude, are you freaking serious? I can't with you right now," India laughed and went to the kitchen to retrieve what Zahara requested. It amazed her how much different stuff her sister craved.

"Here," she handed her a small box. "Aye, where is your packed bag and the stuff you taking with you? I'm about to load up the car then come back for you."

"Good! I can finish these in peace. Everything should already be stacked by alongside the door behind you."

During the ride, all Zahara could do was try to remember the breathing tips she learned in Lamaze class. India drove as fast as her size seven Adidas shoe could press down on the gas pedal. Not much longer from their destination, India pulled into the hospital's emergency entrance. She turned on the hazard signal and quickly hopped out the car. She rushed to open the passenger door then ran inside to get assistance. Two nurses rushed back outside as one pushed a wheelchair. They transported Zahara inside while India moved the car into the parking lot and quickly returned to be by her sister's side.

SET UP IN A HOSPITAL ROOM, Dr. Kid came in to check on Zahara to make sure she was comfortable as possible. India stood alongside watching and listening to everything the nurses and doctor did and said. While they waited for Jacob to arrive, India grew nervous yet excited for the arrival of baby Matthew. Zahara remained in active labor but hadn't dilated past seven centimeters yet.

"I never thought you would be the one to have a baby first. Are you ready for this lifelong challenge?"

"Girl, at this point I don't have a choice," Zahara said joking. "For real though, I'm scared but ready to meet my prince. Life is so crazy sis because I never thought I would be a mom. Please vow that you will stay by my side and help me. We must make sure Matthew doesn't grow up like we did. This kid will be loved without a doubt."

"Sis, I will always be here for you and my nephew. We are all we have, so we gotta stick together. I'm here forever, sis. Love ya," she said and kissed her sister on the forehead.

"Aww, thanks sis, I love you too! I hope Jacob get here soon. He cannot miss the birth of his son." Zahara changed the topic and India did her best not to comment as she thought about Pastor Thomas.

"Hey! Did I miss anything?" Jacob popped inside the room, giving India a reason to temporarily step out.

"I'm glad you made it. You haven't missed anything yet. I'm still dilating, but the pain is starting to increase. I think it's almost time. AHH!" she screamed. She pressed the call button in need of a nurse. "Jacob, I can't believe we will be parents to a precious little boy in the next few hours. I cannot believe it."

"Yes, God is so awesome!"

"Hi, Ms. Hudson, how are you doing?"

"I feel the pain and pressure in my back. When am I supposed to start pushing?"

"PLEASE DON'T PUSH! Let me get the doctor. Hang in there, honey. Your precious baby is ready."

India finally appeared again just in time to be by her sister's side. The sisters held hands and waited for the doctor. Zahara's cried and moaned periodically as the pain increased. The pain and agony started to get the best of her. However, she wanted a natural childbirth.

"Okay, I hear it's time. I'm Dr. Kid, that is Megan and Monica, and we're going to make sure your delivery goes smoothly. Let me see what's going on here." He lifted the sheet that covered her and sure enough the cervix completely opened. "Alright, folks let's deliver a baby!"

Suddenly India began to look peeked around the eyes as if she would be sick and it was obvious to everyone in the room. Zahara wanted her to be in the room but didn't get mad because she couldn't.

"Sis, I love you dearly, but I can't stay and watch this. I'm gonna be sick. I'll be right outside promise."

Once India left the room, everyone stood in their place ready to play their role to bring Matthew into the world. Zahara grabbed Jacob's hand and squeezed it tightly as the pain increased.

"Okay Ms. Hudson, I'm going to need you to only push when I tell you to, but from the looks of things, your son is ready to come out.

Zahara felt the pain ease up as the baby's head emerged out. She pushed and strained in between breathing. Jacob tried to do all he could to cheer her on and wipe her forehead.

"Okay, stop!" Dr. Kid said while he removed some of the amniotic fluid from the nose and mouth. "You're doing good, Ms. Hudson. Your baby is almost here!"

Ready to pass out, she had grown so exhausted from pushing a watermelon from her vajayjay. The childbirth experience turned out to be what she thought it would. Upon the last push, Dr. Kid successfully delivered a healthy boy. In awe, Zahara and Jacob fell in love with their son.

"Welcome to the world, Matthew Hudson Thomas! I'm your mommy, and I love you already." She kissed him on the forehead and then gently handed him to the nurse. While she laid still her breathing resumed back to normal, but the pain persisted intensely. She squeezed Jacob's hand again.

"What's wrong?" Concerned Jacob attentively observed her flushed face

"I feel dizzy baby. What's wrong with me?"

Immediately, Jacob yelled, "DR. KID, SOMETHING IS WRONG! HELP!"

He and the nurse rushed over to tend to Zahara who had lost unconsciousness. Never did it occur to her or anyone else that a complication would arise during it all. Beside himself, Jacob paced unable to comprehend what had just happened. Suddenly the sound of the machines began to rapidly beep until the flatline tone filled his ears.

"NOOOO! GOD PLEASE DON'T!" Jacob cried out because he knew something was not right. Zahara was not responsive nor did her body react to anything the doctor and nurses did.

"Mr. Thomas, I have to ask you to step out for a minute. I promise to come out and talk with you momentarily."

14

JACOB THOMAS

A piece of Jacob went with Zahara the day she died minutes after giving birth. He never believed life would be given and taken all at the same time. Broken and beyond in shock he tried to function, but it didn't do any good. A freak tragedy, his pain reflected in his everyday interactions with people. His colleagues at CNT offered their condolences as they too were saddened by Zahara's death. Jacob's boss allowed him to take some personal time in agreement to return when he felt ready.

Almost a week had passed yet time seemed to stand still causing Jacob to remain withdrawn. He camped out in the basement like a hermit, shamed and embarrassed, not able to face Michelle or his son. Jacob cried until there were no tears left. He mourned for his mistress so much so that he never considered Michelle's feelings. While he wallowed on the couch, he suddenly had an epiphany. Jacob began to realize how blessed he was to have a caring and compassionate woman in his life.

As a wife, Michelle did something very few women would. She raised a love child and opened her home to the mistress' sister. It was in that moment he had a newfound respect and appreciation for his wife and women in general. He recalled when the baby first arrived home with the two of them. He clearly had no clue about parenting. Beyond thankful for the gentle hearted woman he married, Jacob did everything possible to make things right with her.

Time didn't heal all wounds, but Jacob learned to cope with his loss by working and spending all spare time with family. Family had become a priority to him, which surprised Michelle. Impressed with his change, Jacob tried to show Michelle that he meant what he said about doing better to repair their broken home. As a parent, he had to let go of the selfish ways in order to grow into the honest man he used to be. Unfortunately, it took death to make him come to his senses. It only goes to show that only God has the final word.

Soon after, he returned to his regular busy schedule, which kept him away a few days per week. Although he loved being a father, at times it grew hard to be around Matthew because he resembled Zahara so much. Eventually Jacob learned that no matter how much time he spent away from Matthew, he'd always resemble his mother.

He and Michelle worked things out, but their marriage remained on the rocks. Not at the intimate phase of their marriage, he took a lot of cold showers and constantly read his bible to resist temptations. Slowly but surely, Jacob improved without the help of medication. He eventually gave it another go behind the pulpit, and to his surprise, agreed to preach once a month. A spark lit up inside of him, something from deep within that reintroduced the Jacob Thomas he was before Zahara. He'd came to the realization that life wouldn't wait on him nor would he be forgiven unless he repented.

"Good morning Jacob," a female voice whispered in his ear. He slowly rolled from his side to his back to find Michelle standing by the bedside.

"Michelle?" he questioned eyes partially opened. "What time is it?

"It's me Jacob, and it's five-thirty. Hey, sit up. We need to talk before I get ready for church," she insisted and sat at the edge of the bed.

"Did I do something wrong?" he inquired while he sat up and leaned his back against the pillow and headboard unsure what she was about to say. Whatever it was he prayed it brought good news instead of the opposite.

"Look a lot has happened, and we both have been able to act accordingly for Matthew's sake. Everything that has happened made me realize how short life is. Love is more powerful than hate, so I officially forgive you."

"Michelle, please forgive me for putting you through all of this mess. I'm obviously not perfect, but I'm trying to redeem myself. I miss you and how things used to be. I miss sharing laughs, thoughts, and intimacy. I miss us," he confessed whole heartily.

"I do too. Slowly we can work to become better spouses and parents. I'm not making any promises, but for now, you can return to our bedroom, only if you want to," Michelle offered.

"GOD IS GOOD!" Jacob shouted.

"Don't get so happy, mister," she said.

"I'm grateful. Thankful!"

"Okay, I gotta go feed the baby and get ready for church. Get your butt up, no more moping around. What would Jesus do?"

"Really?" he cocked his head to the side.

"What?" she grinned then busted out in laughter.

He watched her stand up and sashay away as if she knew his eyes were glued to her backside. Jacob shook his head and let out a chuckle in disbelief of their chat while he climbed out of bed. Michelle had given him the motivation needed to get showered and dressed. He even cleaned his living space in the basement. By the time he made it up the stairs to the first floor, the sun had just begun to rise. The large bay windows were the perfect view for such a beautiful sight.

While Michelle remained on the second floor, he decided to get breakfast started. After all, it was the gesture that counted. Besides he was hungry enough to eat good. Jacob moved around the kitchen with ease as he prepared two ham and cheese omelets, fluffy butter-milk biscuits, and a small bowl with mixed fruit on the side.

Just as Michelle made her way down the stairs with Matthew, India knocked on the back door before she let herself in. She did the same thing each morning unless the Thomas asked her to phone first. Jacob agreed with Michelle that India deserved a key and access to Matthew.

"Morning! God is good," India praised as she closed the door.

"And all the time God is good," Jacob quoted back. "Look at you ready to go praise the Lord. You look really nice."

India exclaimed, "Yes!"

"Morning, India. I pray all is well your way," Michelle greeted her with a side hug then leaned over to tend to Matthew who sat in his Fisher Price frog floor seat.

"Are you eating?" Jacob questioned.

Almost a quarter to nine, Jacob served breakfast to everyone and cleaned up the kitchen afterwards. Michelle finished the final touches of her makeup, brushed her teeth, and gathered her belong-ings. Jacob opted out of attending church, not in the mood to be around people. Instead, India left with Michelle leaving Jacob to bond with his son.

Homebound, Jacob stayed with Matthew and watched preseason football while Michelle praised the Lord at church. During that bonding time, Jacob held Matthew in his lap and talked to him as if he understood every word.

"Hey, lil man! How you doing? You look just like your mom." Matthew just grinned and kicked his legs.

Jacob stared at Matthew as he cooed and looked at him with those slanted eyes. It hurt knowing Zahara had to miss out on their child growing up. It amazed him how much had changed since June. He bounced Matthew on his lap and continued to talk baby talk.

"Your mama would've loved you so much! You, my son, are a special child. May the Lord bless and keep you," he prayed. After-wards the two shared more laughs, baby talk, and of course, Jacob took pictures.

HOME FOR DINNER the four gathered at the table in fellowship until Michelle phone rang. Of course, she tried to ignore it not wanting to leave her family, but duty called as she had to rush off to the hospital. India stayed long enough to help clean and say goodnight to her precious nephew. Jacob and India had gotten along really well, but at times, she resembled Zahara. That played tricks with his mind, and sometimes, it even tempted him with impure thoughts.

"Alright Jacob, I'm headed out now. Have a good evening and call if you need me," India stated.

"I sure will. Thank you for everything, India. We appreciate you," he confided in her.

"Have a good night," she said and closed the door behind her. Jacob put up the palm of his hand to gesture. He shook his head as if he tried to shake the bad thoughts out.

15

MICHELLE THOMAS

Occupied by thoughts of lust, Michelle feared the Lord would punish her for her recent actions with the deacon. Dinner with the deacon went perfect, and he remained a gentleman. Although the physical restraints were obvious between them, he verbally told her how he felt not holding anything back. In a nutshell, he confessed that switching churches was a mistake. He went on to reveal the true nature of his dinner invite, which was to become intimate. In shock that he finally confessed, she too shared his feelings, but as a pastor, it just wasn't right. Two glasses of wine later, a vulnerable Michelle found herself in the arms of another man. The way he held and kissed her passionately made her forget all about Jacob.

Despite not having intercourse, Michelle crossed a line that made her no better than Jacob. She broke her own rule, and although her actions weren't for revenge, they went against the bible. In desperate need to make amends for her sin, she prayed and vowed to invest in the first individual who phoned her. Be her luck the Lord worked in mysterious ways and answered her prayer as her phone rang. Caller ID displayed on the screen as she answered.

"Pastor Michelle speaking."

"Hi pastor, this is India. Do you remember me?"

"Yes, I do. What's going on? You sound shaken up," she asked out of concern.

"I'm at the hospital and my sister...my sister is dead." India busted out crying.

"What hospital? I'm on my way. Just hold on, baby girl." Michelle broke into action mode. She held the phone between her ear and shoulder as she grabbed an ink pen.

"Third floor. Please hurry!" India cried out.

Michelle prayed during her drive for God to wrap his arms around India as she mourned. She had taken a liking to India and felt it was her responsibility to look after her more now than ever. When she arrived at the hospital, Michelle quickly rushed to console India when she came face to face with Jacob. The awkwardness created a tense moment. Unconsciously aware, a tear rolled down each cheek as she realized Zahara had been the sister India mentioned.

"Jacob," she spoke and acknowledged with a quick head nod. Michelle couldn't believe God provided the most challenging hurdle in front of her. The individuals who caused her pain now relied on her kindness, and it deemed her debt to pay.

Confused by her presence, Jacob tried to find the words to say to his wife who had come to console the sister of his mistress. "Hi, Michelle. You are the last person I expected to see. How did you find out?"

"I called her," India spoke up. She shifted and put a little distance between the three before she continued.

"Your wife has been of great support to me even before all of this. You see I knew about the affair, and I felt bad for Pastor Thomas, so I showed up at the church. It bothered me what my sister was doing, and I had to meet the woman who didn't deserve the betrayal. I'm sorry, please forgive me," she pleaded.

"Wow! Talk about a suspenseful day. Well, none of that matters now," Michelle voiced.

"What am I'm going to do now? I'm so lost right night," India mumbled as Michelle looked upon.

"You can come home with me. I have enough space for you to have *privacy all while not being alone. At the end of the day, we are family. Therefore you're coming with me," Michelle stated.*

At that moment it was plain as day that prayers sent up to our creator were surely answered. The Lord sent Michelle to the hospital blind sighted just to test her promise to repent and make up for sin with Deacon Jones.

ALL SHE COULD DO WAS PRAISE the Lord for his blessings that rained down upon her and her family. Michelle, Jacob, and India formed an awkward relationship all for the sake of Matthew. The three adults set aside their differences and made a promise to raise Zahara's son. India even went as far as moving closer to the Thomas' so that she could see her nephew daily. It had been a horrible ordeal, Zahara's death, which left a baby without a mother. Regardless of Michelle's feelings towards her for sleeping with Jacob, she never wished death on her.

Michelle never dreamed nor desired to be a mother the way it happened. However, she was forever grateful. Unable to bear children remained a tough pill for her to swallow. When the situation presented itself, she took on the responsibility like a good Christian. Often Michelle selfishly thought Zahara's death was not in vain, but instead, a blessing to her for enduring the pain Jacob and Zahara had caused.

Nonetheless, her bond with India grew over time bringing them closer and closer. Still broken by her sister's death, Michelle did her best to fill that void India lost. However, it was Matthew who helped her heal. Matthew resembled his mother in the eyes but had Jacob's facial features.

Things in the home changed drastically with Jacob and a child living there, but she adjusted. After constantly praying, Michelle's change of heart included allowing Jacob back into their bedroom. A part of her still loved him despite it all. The Christian in her made room for forgiveness. She learned time waited for no one, so the blended family worked daily to be one. Michelle even gave India a key to the house for emergencies specifically. India spent time at their home daily to spend time with and assist with Matthew.

LATER THAT NIGHT while Matthew sat quietly and watched *Paw Patrol,* Michelle worked on her home MacBook. Jacob was away in Memphis at a retreat for a few days. Things between the two improved, but awkward moments presented itself when it came to the baby boy.

Michelle put Matthew to bed a little after eight at night and prayed he slept through the night. She had a lot of reading and preparing to do and needed the quietness to focus. Just as she sat down in front of her computer, a knock at the door grabbed her attention. Not expecting anyone, she was a little unsure who could be at her door that late at night. India always called or texted when she was on the way. Before she opened the door, she peeped out the window and noticed a detective car. Her heart began to beat uncontrollably and as a heat wave of nervousness swept over her. She quickly opened the door to find a black and white officer standing before her.

"Oh my god, what happened? Is it my husband? Why are you here?" Her emotions soon got the best of her as she thought the worst.

"Ma'am calm down. Are you Michelle Thomas?" the tall, black officer asked me.

He pulled out his badge and flashed it before tucking it back in his pocket, his partner did the same thing. Still nervous, I stood and blinked while in shock to have the law at my door.

"Yes. Can you please tell me what's going on," she pleaded as her stomach fluttered.

"Ma'am, may we come inside? We need to ask you a few questions about Nikki Thomas."

"Come in, I'm sorry, where are my manners," she said and moved to the side allowing the men to enter her home. She showed them to the sitting room as they all sat at the same time. The officer continued where he left off with the basic routine questions before he delivered the agonizing news.

"With confirmation that we are talking about the same person, I'm sorry to inform you that your sister was found deceased last night."

"Oh no, I knew something would happen. I begged her to be careful because some people were evil." She wept but did her best to hold in her pain until the officers left.

"Apparently a fight or scuffle between Nikki and a guy she had been with that night. From what we've gathered thus far, umm, your-"

"Yes, she was once a he," Michelle admitted boldly saving the officer the embarrassment of saying it aloud. "It was something we feuded about, and I did my best to accept her choice. Not all people accepted folks like my sister who battled within."

"Bystanders confirm the two had some heated words and one thing led to another. The man forcefully punched her, which caused her to fall. Her head slammed on the pavement. Doctors say the cause of death was a subdural hematoma."

"Oh, my goodness," she cried out then put her hand over her mouth. Regretful that her sister died alone, the guilt filled Michelle as the pit of her stomach reacted.

"Well, Mrs. Thomas, we will be in touch and will need you to come identify the body. I know it's never a good time for death, but you will have to claim the body and contact the funeral home. Here is my card."

Michelle took the card as the three moved towards the front door. Numb from the news, it hadn't sunk in yet. The officers displayed their empathy for her the entire time. When she opened the door, the first detective made a slow exit.

"If you hear or think of anything that would help us, call without hesitation."

"Of course. So, is the body at the morgue or funeral home?"

"At the morgue right now until you have a funeral home pick her up,"

Once the door closed, Michelle slid down to the floor and let her head fall into her hands. She had finally come to terms and accepted Nikki's choice to live life as a female. When Zahara died, Michelle let go and let God guide her down the road of acceptance. This situation differed because Nikki was flesh in blood.

As a pastor, she knew better than to judge anyone for their choices, which included family. The two were close growing up but grew apart as the got older and older. On the floor, she thought back to when they were no more than seven years old and played dress up. It was that moment she assumed Nick knew that he was different from the other boys. He liked to dress up a little more than he should have, walking in heels and wearing the big pretty hats.

She had consoled many during their time of grief, given countless eulogies, and attended funreals. The feelings were so different because her sibling no longer existed in the physical sense. Pain caused by death affected people differently and Michelle tended to manage it well until now. Flooded with memories, she regretted the time they didn't talk or hang out together.

Another knock at the door made Michelle quickly wipe away her tears as she got up from the floor. She turned the doorknob and opened it. "Come in," Michelle motioned and closed the door behind India. The two women moved towards the sitting room and just as she attempted to sit on the sofa, Matthew's cries glared through the baby monitor.

"I'll go check on him! Take a seat and sit back," India insisted then proceeded up the staircase.

Glad to have India over, Michelle needed to share her tragic news but feared it at the same time. Although it had been five months since Zahara's death, the topic was very sensitive.

"How is Matthew?"

"I got him back to sleep. All he needed was a diaper change and a little lullaby."

"Wonderful. He sleeps great at night, thank goodness," Michelle added.

"Okay, so what were the police doing here? You know I'm nosy."

"Well, it was about my sister and umm..."

"What?"

"She is dead. Some guy hit her so hard that the fall to the ground caused instant death. It is crazy because we had just started back talking again."

"No. I'm so sorry to hear that. Know I'm here for you just as you were for me. That is horrible."

"Tell me about it. I can still remember when we were little and played without a care in the world. Those were such good times full of laughs. It's crazy how memories are all I have now."

"I've learned that anything is possible and up until my nephew was born, my beliefs were torn. I now believe there has to be a higher power. It is because of you and my sister's death that life has a different meaning."

Pleased to hear India finally admit she believed in God had to be the most comforting feeling. The two shared a sentimental moment neither of them expected, which only displayed how unexpected life could be. Only God knew the outcome for Michelle and India. A great loss such as that of a sibling never went away despite the amount of time that passed.

India ended up sleeping over on the couch because she didn't want to leave Michelle alone. Her way to pay it forward involved helping around the house with cooking meals and looking after Matthew. Michelle had to deal with funeral arrangements not to mention run her church so to have India saved her stress. India did what she could around the house.

When Jacob returned from traveling and learned of the recent event, his acts of kindness went above and beyond. He made sure to verbally tell Michelle she wasn't alone during her mourning and even paid for everything that didn't get covered by insurance. Jacob hated to see his wife grieve, so he tried to console her in any way that he could. India even volunteered to help around the house and church to free Michelle from worry.

16

JACOB THOMAS

T he Thomas family prepared for their first major holiday together, which included India. Jacob and India fell into a brief depression with the absence of Zahara, and Michelle missed her dear sister Nikki. All three went through a phase where the pain of their loss prompted them to act in a peculiar manner.

Jacob gained a habit of having a nightcap the minute India put Matthew down at night. She had such a gift with her nephew that Jacob wanted her to continue that bond. Michelle never objected and, in fact, made sure Matthew knew India. In preparation for church activities, Michelle spent a little more time at church leaving Jacob at home to serve as Mr. Mom. In addition, his work began to suffer due to his lack of love for the camera.

Michelle's absence bothered Jacob fearing similar results would arise again. His fear stemmed from the fact that India had become so comfortable that she dressed a certain way, which made Jacob uncomfortable. India was very attractive, and there were moments he saw Zahara in her, which triggered inappropriate thoughts. He quoted Matthew 26:41 daily, but it did no good as he resorted in other unhealthy alternatives. The once well-respected pastor and esteemed talk show host had succumbed to depression, porn, and Scotch.

ALMOST TWO WEEKS before Thanksgiving Jacob's secret obsession grew and his battle within intensified. Although Michelle let him move back into their bedroom, he hadn't had sex in over five months. That type of backup nearly drove him insane as he stayed held up in the basement bathroom watching *PornHub*. In an effort to cover his tracks, he'd pretend to be working on small projects that required privacy. Therefore, India spent more time in their home than her own.

Imagine Jacob's surprise when he'd been notified Michelle planned to travel for church related purposes. She informed Jacob and India of her three-day trip and his fear to be left alone with India came true. In fact, the day Michelle left, he encouraged India to take Matthew for the night, and without any objections she did. He didn't trust himself to be left that long with another woman that he had grown attracted to sexually.

The following night, however, the devil played tag causing both Jacob and India to walk the thin line. Around ten Saturday night India put Matthew down like clockwork and said her goodbyes to Jacob. Once he locked up and checked the baby monitor, he poured up a drink. He turned up the double shot of Scotch then poured up another repeating again. Unable to realize why he needed the alcohol, he flopped on the couch making sure to keep the monitor nearby.

Unexpectedly he heard a lite tap on the door then it pushed opened by the time he had gotten up. Each day he watched India enter and exit the home and wondered what life would've been like if Zahara was alive. He visualized her waltzing through the door greeting him with a kiss, them making love, and living a happy life. The scent of India's sweet perfume caused him to snap back.

"Jacob, I'm so sorry to just come in like that but something seems to be wrong with my hot water. May I take a shower here please?" she questioned.

"Ah yeah, that should be fine. Help yourself since you practically live here anyway. While you're at it, you might as well sleep here too. It doesn't make sense to go outside fresh out the water," Jacob commented.

"If you insist, thank you," she said and ran up the stairs.

Jacob waited a few minutes before he went upstairs curious to know if India showered with the door opened or not. Just as he suspected, it was open, and he caught a glimpse of her naked body through the glass shower door. Before he could disappear, she had turned around and caught him. He watched her jump as she tried to cover herself.

"Shit!" he blurted as he reverted to the bedroom that he shared with Michelle. He wondered if India planned on telling or keeping what happened a secret.

"So, you get off by peeping in showers, freak!" she spat at Jacob.

"India, I'm so sorry I swear that wasn't my intention. I was walking past and noticed how beautiful you were. I guess you made me think about your sister," he confessed. Embarrassed he assumed she would cuss him out and threaten to tell Michelle but ironically something else happened.

"I'm not my sister! I wish I knew what it was about her that made men go nuts for her. Men have never drooled over me until now, and yet again it's because of Zahara."

Jacob grew confused by her sudden meltdown because until then he painted her to be a good girl who remained reserved and quiet. The woman wrapped in a towel who stood before him had shown another side. Just when Jacob thought the worst had occurred India dropped her towel. His eyes roamed over her B-cup lady lumps and the lightly shaved sweet spot between her legs. He took a mental note of the exact moment unable to speak as he stared her down.

"You liked what you saw earlier, and now it's up close and personal. This is your one and only time to take advantage of this moment. I get it you miss my sister, so since I'm such a resemblance to Zahara, do to me what you have dreamed of doing. I've noticed you watching me."

"Why haven't you said anything before?"

"Because it's wrong, and I didn't want to make a move and have it backfired in my face. However, at this very moment, we both need something from each other, and I'm willing to give it to you. It's been so long since I've felt a man's touch," she said while rubbing her hand down his chest.

She persisted to unbutton Jacob's shirt, as he could no longer restrain his hands from caressing her soft skin. Anxious, he assisted in stripping out of his clothes no longer able to fight the urge.

"No! We can't do this," he murmured.

"WHAT?" India said disappointedly.

"I mean we can't do this in here. Michelle will kill us. We have to go in the basement," he suggested. In heat, the two quickly moved to the basement ready to test drive each other's equipment. Jacob craved the very essence of her not able to wait as he scooped her up in his arms.

"Lord, please forgive us," he faintly whispered as he laid India on her back.

His lips kissed every inch of her glistening brown skin that smelled like cocoa butter. The visions he had didn't do justice compared to his up close and personal view of her beautiful, womanly gift. The glare from the night light helped him feel under the mattress as he retrieved a condom and slipped it on before entering India.

"Ahh... This feels good! Wow, I can't believe this is happening," Jacob moaned.

With each stroke, he stared into her eyes unable to describe the multiple emotions he felt shoot through his body. Her direct stare back proved she too had shared some of his frustrations. Doing wrong felt so right to him that he temporarily imagined it was Zahara in the bed.

"Ahh, I've missed this so much, baby! This can't be real. Oh yes, this is so good," he groaned again.

India's body moved with his; their motion replicated that of two people who shared a moment of lust. Just as Jacob finished up, something weird happened that was unexplainable.

"I'm about to come," he murmured. The two then let out a sound that indicated relief. "Ahh, that was amazing Z," he professed. India propped herself up on her left arm and faced him. He realized he had called her by the wrong name, but instead of cursing him out, she simply replied.

"I'll agree it was great, smooth daddy!"

Jacob jumped out of bed and hit the light switch as if he heard or saw a ghost, which caused India to jump up too. The lit-up room revealed the two naked individuals who had just betrayed Michelle and Zahara. Reality had hit them as Jacob began to get dressed quickly.

"What's wrong? What happened that fast?" she questioned out of confusion.

"You called me smooth daddy. Nobody but your sister called me that after we, you know," he said spooked.

Unsure if he had officially lost his mind, there hadn't been an explanation. Unable to explain it, India went upstairs to check in on Matthew while he remained in the room. He showered, changed the sheets, and went to bed questioning his sanity only to wake up the morning to another surprise.

"Jacob! Hey, sleepyhead, wake up," the woman's voice echoed. Like deja-vu, he turned over to find Michelle standing over him like the last time. He jumped up and almost out of his skin.

"Michelle," he said as if he didn't recognize his surroundings. "I thought you were supposed to be gone for another day."

"Yes, we were, but Deacon Jones had a family emergency, so we were able to get back early. Plus, the holiday is less than forty-eight hours away, and we all got some cooking to do. Did anything exciting happen?"

"Not a thing! I decided to move back down here until I'm officially worthy to be on the second level," he asserted.

"Oh. What does that mean?"

"I just need more time to get my head right. A lot has happened you know, too much to digest, but thank you for the kind gesture."

"I understand. More than you would believe," she replied.

THE BEEPING SOUND of the smoke detector went off because of Jacob who burnt the cornbread. Luckily, India walked in just in time to whip up another pan. Michelle had called to inform them she'd be thirty minutes. Alone for the time being, he did everything possible to keep at least a three feet distance between the two. Despite his move back to the basement, their intimate moment had been forever engraved inside his head.

Thanksgiving was a day of giving thanks, yet Jacob found himself weighed down by guilt. He didn't feel worthy as he sat next to Michelle knowing what he and India had done days prior. Rather than ruffle feathers, he held onto the secret that he knew for sure would end the Thomas family. Little did he know, every saint has a secret, including his holier than thou pastor wife.

TO BE CONTINUED

CPSIA information can be obtained
at www.ICGtesting.com
Printed in the USA
LVHW111744120220
646719LV00006B/1145